# PRIDEAUX

# GHOST

# STORIES

FEATURING THE PRIDEAUXS OF

HARFORD, STOWFORD

AND ERMINGTON

A CIP catalogue record for this title is

Available from the British Library.

ISBN 978-09954609-2-8


www.paganuspublishing.co.uk

First Published in 2016


**Paganus Publishing**

Ruthin

Denbighshire

*Paganus Publishing*

# DEDICATION

This book is dedicated to Richard Fulke Paganus Prideaux.

# AUTHOR

A A Prideaux has horses and dogs and lives in Wales.

# FOREWORD

Followers of the blogs on my website and readers of my books such as **A Ghost Story, A Christmas Story** and **The Bishop and The Witch**, will know that I have already written much about my branch of the Prideaux clan.

I possess detailed information of each ancestor Prideaux, either already made public or still in my own records. These people all lived and died in the towns, villages and properties I describe.  They experienced the events I write about. I have walked the same roads and visited the same properties as these Prideauxs used to do.  The spooky connection is a mixture of oral tradition and artistic licence.

This series of Prideaux short stories, those already published and the subsequent several (I have 28 stories to tell) all feature the Prideaux experience and interaction with horror and the paranormal.

**Prideaux Ghost Stories** features John, (the son of John in **A Ghost Story)**, his son Thomas and his grandson Thomas.

The Dartmoor Witch – John Prideaux.
John and Agnes meet a witch on Dartmoor and seal their eternal fate. They encounter the hooded man and other ghosts who follow the family throughout their lives.

Stowford Demons – Thomas Prideaux.
Thomas and his family not only suffer through the Puritan uprising and bigotry but encounter the hooded man as the county veers towards Civil War.


The Ermington Curse – Thomas Prideaux.
Thomas has experienced severe stress and become irrecoverably damaged following his father's death, the Civil War and the family's loss of fortune. The ghosts of dead soldiers and the mysterious hooded man all conspire to cast a dark shadow over his life.

# CAST LIST

I thought it might help you follow the many Thomases and Johns featuring in these Prideaux stories. All of the characters lived and all are ancestors of mine. If this work had been about fictional people, then I would have used a larger variety of names for clarity. However, they were all real and so the least I can do is give them their own names. The history written about is correct, but the ghost stories I include in each story – there are many yet to be published – have only been passed down through oral tradition.

**Dartmoor Witch**

John Prideaux was the son of John Prideaux who featured in my book **A Ghost Story.**
He was born in 1540 and married Agnes (related to the Williams family of Stowford.)
Their children were;

Thomas born 1571
Johan born 1573
Agnes born 1574
Henry born 1575
John born 1578
Hugh born 1580
Christopher born 1582
Richard born 1583

Francis born 1584
Elizabeth born 1586

The Williams Family;

Adam Williams married Alice Prideaux in 1510. They had a son and daughter – Thomas and Katherine.
Thomas Williams (Speaker to Elizabeth I) married Emlyn Drwe and they had 6 children including their heir, John.

## Stowford Demons

Thomas Prideaux was born in 1571 and married Blanche. Their children were;

John born 1605
Thomas born 1610
Richard born 1611
Hugh born 1612
Susan born 1614
James born 1618

**Ermington Curse**

Thomas Prideaux was born in 1610 and married Joane.
Their children were;

James born 1647
Andrew born 1649
Peter born 1651

Many of the characters were christened, married and buried
at Harford Church or at Ermington and Modbury.

Prepare yourself – they are all called Peter in the next book...

# CONTENTS

# THE DARTMOOR WITCH

## Featuring John and Agnes Prideaux of Stowford

This Stowford party had been anticipated for weeks.

Following years of religious uncertainty and persecution, recently there had been a period of peace in the country. Emlyn Williams told those who would listen that it was because Queen Elizabeth had been getting rid of anyone whom she considered to be her enemy. Emlyn's father-in-law Thomas Williams had been a Speaker of the House of Commons until his tragic and sudden death. With this familial backing she considered herself an oracle on all things political. She probably was, she knew enough of the 'right' people.

"As soon as that Scottish woman is dead, the Queen will feel safe and the rest of us will be able to get on with our own lives," Great Aunt Alice Williams announced to her Devonian niece, Agnes.

"I don't like all this killing and the constant executions under the pretence of treason and crimes against God," Agnes answered forcefully.

"I should keep that opinion to yourself, my dear," advised her aunt.

Agnes bobbed a dutiful curtsey in acknowledgement and skipped off to her friends. At 18 years old, Agnes was feeling the need to marry quickly before she lost her looks. She was used to living with privilege and had no intention of marrying out of it. This wonderful party at Stowford Hall was a treat and she was going to take full advantage. Her Great Aunt, Alice Williams had promised the women several eligible men and she had promised the men several beautiful and well-connected women.

Both Emlyn and Alice Williams were good at throwing parties when they felt the time was right and everyone who was anyone would attend.

The young women stood together collectively giggling and gossiping, albeit in full view of their chaperones, who casually sat in nearby chairs.

"Who is that?" asked Agnes of her friend Johanna.

"That is John Prideaux. He is related to your Aunt Emlyn, so I suppose he must be related to you somehow," her friend answered. "He lives very near to us in Stowford."

"Who is the girl making eyes at him?"

"That is Anna Fortescue. I think she has quite a bit of money coming to her. Why? Do you like the look of him?"

"Liking the look and going to get him."

Agnes had the determined expression on her face with which Johanna was so familiar.

"Bad luck Miss Fortescue, you just lost a competition you did not even know you were in," said Johanna, grabbing hold of her friend's arm.

The girls laughed out loud, causing some of the women at the gathering to tut-tut their disapproval. John Prideaux looked across at them and smiled at Agnes.

"Round one to moi," she said.

"I can tell you some things about that young lady that she would not expect anyone here to know," whispered Johanna.

"Tell me, tell me!" squealed Agnes.

Agnes Williams was a well-heeled cousin of the Williams family of Devon. It was her Aunt Emlyn Williams, a wealthy landowner with acres of property in Stowford, who was throwing this party for her neighbours.

Emlyn had been married to Thomas Williams. Recently widowed and often bored, she enjoyed her matchmaking and socialising. Thomas's father Adam had bought up large tracts of land following the dissolution of the monasteries. Thomas Williams then purchased more land to become an even wealthier man than his father.

Adam Williams married Alice Prideaux who turned out to be a great financial advisor and knew how to make money. When Thomas, their son became a favourite of Queen Elizabeth in his role as Speaker, he was rewarded with the demesne lands between Stowford Manor and Prideaux House to the south of Dartmoor. The Queen gave these 100 acres of former royal hunting ground to him and his heirs forever.

The farms and properties which accompanied these lands were now the responsibility of Thomas to manage. During his many absences in London, he left the management in the capable hands of his mother Alice and his wife Emlyn.   When Thomas died in 1566, two years prior to this party following a fall from his horse while out hunting. Emlyn Williams continued her management and looked after the tenants and the lands, working as hard as she ever had.

Parties such as the one these young people attended happened often around the County and were an excellent place for the young and the widowed to meet the right sort of person. The Williams family often used them as fundraisers, either in cash or in kind. They were very successful social and charitable occasions. The son and heir of Thomas and Emlyn was still a teenager but allowed to attend this party. Although Thomas had not approved of his son or his raucous behavior, Thomas's will revealed that he had nevertheless ensured in law that his son John was his heir. John, even after learning of his new responsibilities was still a wastrel and cared little about Stowford and the family inheritance. Alice and Emlyn needed to keep a constant eye upon him.

Agnes Williams had spent much of her teenage years in Exeter and Bath with extended family and through the friends she met there and the connections she made had learnt behaviours that were not familiar to the inhabitants of the South Hams. Agnes did not intend to let these skills go to waste.

"Agnes my dear, you are looking very thoughtful."

"Aunt Alice! Yes, I have seen the man I intend to marry and was just wondering how to go about getting him."

"I see. Am I allowed to know the name of this man?"

"Yes, John Prideaux. I only just found out his name myself."

"One of my own family! I shall have to see how I can help you, I know his parents well. Thomas was very good friends with his father John. They used to have such fine adventures together. There was this one time when they travelled onto the moor during a snowstorm… But I am sure that would not interest you." The smile on the old lady's face began to falter as she thought of her son. But she rallied and asked,

"Where is he Agnes?"

Agnes pointed to the handsome young man talking to Miss Fortescue.

"I see that he is already occupied. She should not present too much trouble for you young lady. That girl does not look as though she has much fight in her."

Agnes stared at the quiet girl in the beige dress standing next to John Prideaux. Her face was pale and her fair hair and brown eyes were not lighting the room. She compared the girl's image with that of John Prideaux. He was a tall man with dark wavy hair, grown long enough to touch the top of his collar. His complexion was dark and his eyes hazel. The full lips and huge grin which seemed to be permanently fixed showed white teeth which gave the impression of trouble.

"He is just the kind of man I want," Agnes unconsciously said out loud.

"He has made an impression on you darling. Come on, let's get a proper introduction," whispered Great Aunt Alice. She had managed to catch rich Adam Williams and so instantly recognised the determined look in her niece's eyes. It would be fun to help her. There wasn't much fun at 80 years old.

"John. John! Come over here this instant!" Shouting at her grandson was a guaranteed way to get his attention. In spite of the young man's wealth, influence and careless attitude to life, he came meekly over to his grandmother's side. She still had some control over his allowance.

"Yes grandmother, what can I do for you? Do you want another drink? Hello Agnes, are you enjoying yourself?" John said with the attractive charm he used on everyone.

"Don't fuss so John. Now listen to me, you see John Prideaux over there, by the fireplace? I want you to introduce him to Agnes."

John knew better than to ask his grandmother why and so walked towards his guest, returning with him less than a minute later.

"Grandmother, John Prideaux wants to say hello."

"Hello John."

John Prideaux bowed and took the hand of his hostess and kissed it lightly.

"A pleasure as always, Mrs Williams. You are looking beautiful."

Agnes listened to the deep tones of the attractive man and felt her cheeks flush.

"You are very charming Mr. Prideaux but are welcome here nonetheless." She nudged her grandson and John Williams did his duty.

"John, do you know my cousin, Miss Agnes Williams?"

John Prideaux turned his attention to the pretty girl standing next to Alice and rewarded her with his smile.

"I am honoured to meet you, Miss Williams."

Agnes gave a curtsey and lowered her eyes. Then she rose and looked John straight in the eye and smiled back.

John was a little taken aback as he generally expected his close presence to overcome the women he met and make them nervous. He knew he was handsome and that was enough to get him, well – anything he wanted. This girl was different.

"Mr. Prideaux, I understand you are a good rider, perhaps you will be accompanying my cousin at his hunting tomorrow?"

Now why had she asked him that? It sounded too forward and yet she didn't care.

"We often hunt together Miss Williams but I don't suppose you realize that. Agnes is an accomplished rider, John. She also rides far too fast," said her cousin.

John Williams looked at his two friends and then quizzically at his grandmother, who merely smiled. What had his grandmother dragged him into? If John Prideaux thought he was being set up, he would not let him forget it in a hurry.

"Then we shall see you at the meet tomorrow Mr. Prideaux," Agnes said.

"I sincerely hope so," answered John.

"Hello Mrs Williams!"

Anna Fortescue had used her feminine sixth sense and moved swiftly over to the small gathering, where her potential beau was being snared.

"What a wonderful party this is, Mrs Williams. John and I were just saying how much we were enjoying ourselves."

Agnes turned to her rival and said,

"Miss Fortescue, it is a pleasure to finally meet you. I have heard so much about you from my dear friend Johanna Fiennes. You have a mutual friend in Mr. Giles Abson, I believe?"

Anna Fortescue went white but regained her composure quickly.

"I think that Miss Fiennes was a closer friend of his than I was."

"Apparently he still speaks fondly of the times you two spent together. He was most disappointed when you left town so suddenly."

"I cannot think why," she answered shortly. "John, I am feeling rather warm, perhaps we could take some air?" She looked plaintively at John Prideaux.

"Of course Anna, I would not want you to faint in front of everyone. Perhaps you would like to join us Miss Williams? Mrs. Williams what about you? John, please join us. It is a wonderful evening and I saw some stocks in the garden, they should smell sweetly in this warm evening air." John apparently wanted a crowd.

"Thank you Mr. Prideaux, but my stock smelling days are behind me now. You go Agnes and John and show John Prideaux and of course, Miss Fortescue around the gardens," said the old lady, trying and failing to hide a smile.

"Yes Aunt, I shall."

The four of them moved in the direction of the terrace doors but John Prideaux excused himself as they went through the doorway.

"I must just pop somewhere before we walk ladies," he informed them. He winked at his namesake and the two men went to fetch another drink.

The girls carried on into the warm, moonlit night.

"You seem very interested in my John," said Anna.

"I was not aware that he was your John!" Agnes said in a mock surprised tone.

"He is, or soon will be. I prefer that you accept that information and move on to someone else."

Agnes laughed.

"I am sure that Mr. Prideaux is quite capable making up his own mind."

"Perhaps, but I can also make it up for him." Anna looked at Agnes trying to understand what was going on.

"Does he know about the baby?" Agnes swiftly delivered the arrow to her rival's heart.

"No! How do you know about that?" Anna stopped in her tracks.

"Gossip I am afraid. None of us are safe from that. That is why we women must keep ourselves tidy." Agnes suddenly felt guilty. Perhaps she had gone too far and she certainly had no intentions of passing on the gossip.

"I am lost if that becomes public knowledge. Mother is bringing up the boy as her own. Father knows, but wants to keep it secret."

"No one will hear it from me," said Agnes quietly.

They looked each other, so what now?

John Prideaux came out to join them.

"Ladies, ladies. Let's walk to the walled garden, I hear it is beautiful! But what is the matter with you both? The gaiety has gone!"

The two ladies laughed and accompanied their eager companion as he led them to the gardens.

Two days later a maid announced to Agnes that she was required downstairs to attend her aunt. Agnes had been dressing her most recent homemade doll with a lock of her hair and some she had managed to steal from the collar of John Prideaux. She kissed it and lay it down on her pillow next to her nightgown. She finished dressing in her new pale blue gown and made her way into the library where she expected to see Aunt Emlyn.

As Agnes walked into the room, she caught her breath when she saw who was there. It was her Great Aunt Alice sitting grandly by the fireplace and she was accompanied by John Prideaux. Agnes thought her heart would stop, as he turned to face her when she came into the room.

"John has come to ask if you would like to accompany him on a ride Agnes," said the old lady.

"That would be wonderful," Agnes said, deciding immediately not to hide her joy.

"Change your clothes, Agnes and have your maid go with you. I am not having two young people go out with no other companion!"

John smiled at her during the whole conversation and winked as she was dismissed by her aunt. Agnes walked gracefully out of the room but as soon as she was out of sight, she ran back to her own quarters.

"Mary, Mary!" she shouted to her maid. "Get my new riding clothes, we ride out today!"

The two girls were downstairs in fifteen minutes. Instructions had been given to the stables earlier and the horses were outside, ready and waiting. Agnes was to ride her favourite, a beautiful grey horse and her maid a bay. John was already seated on his black stallion and after much chattering and excitement they were all making their way to the moor.

"Not with Miss Fortescue today Mr. Prideaux?" asked Agnes. She was genuinely curious to know how the girl was, as she still felt guilty about letting Anna know that her secret was out in the open.

"She has left the county I am sorry to tell you, Miss Williams. She has gone back to her parents in Cornwall on some urgent family business. I don't think that she will be returning here."

"That is bad news. I enjoyed her company," Agnes answered.

"Let us see if you can enjoy my company as much," he said.

She noticed that even his eyes smiled and his voice was deep and consequently very attractive to Agnes. Dolly was working her charm back in the bedroom.

She suddenly galloped away from him and was pleased when she saw that he was chasing her. John was surprised to see that catching Agnes was not as easy as he had imagined. Mary the maid, remembering her instructions, wisely held back her pony in a jogtrot.

The two raced onto Dartmoor and made their way towards the highest peaks, passing the ancient stone monuments on the way. John always felt that the vibrations coming from these stones seemed to give them a life of their own.

Today the weather was excellent with a cloudless sky and views for miles. They both knew that this place could become treacherous within minutes if the mist rolled in and the unsuspecting rider or walker became lost. Deaths had occurred in such a way on many occasions in the past.

"Look over there!" shouted John. The two eased up their horses and saw a lone wolf on top of a rocky crag looking back at them. The horses had disturbed partridge which squawked their protest as they flew towards the wolf.

"I wonder why he is out in the daylight without any cover?" asked Agnes, though with no hint of nerves.

"I should imagine that he is hunting food for his cubs. He will ignore us. He has more than enough to eat without attacking us." John said.

They watched for a few minutes, their horses pawing the ground.  In their current view were the wolf, partridge, buzzards, sheep, ponies, cattle, and boars. The flora too in this supposedly bleak place was manifold and beautiful.

"I love this place," said Agnes. "We are so lucky to be here. I want to live here forever."

John looked at her lovely profile appreciating the scenery he had loved from a boy and thought that he would not mind spending a lot of time with this girl.

"We are very lucky," he answered.

They rode further into the moors going north when suddenly they came upon an old cottage which stood completely alone. The cottage was stone built and surrounded by several dilapidated stone outbuildings which appeared to be used as storehouses and shelters for animals. Smoke spiraled from the chimney showing that the cottage was occupied. A small dog came out to greet them, barking a couple of times, but it soon stopped and began to wag its little tail.

"Hello! Is there anyone there?" shouted John.

There was no answer and so interest aroused, he dismounted and went to the door.

"Hello!" he shouted again. Then turning to Agnes he said, "I haven't noticed this place before."

Agnes watched him walk in and after a few moments come out again.

"Jump down Agnes, the lady who lives here has kindly offered us some refreshment."

"How kind," she said and jumped from her horse. Neither thought it unusual that she should do this without assistance. Both instinctively realized how independent the other one was. They moved their horses into a walled area which had water and grazing and Agnes followed John into the cottage.

Inside it was very dark and warm, almost stuffy. The table was covered in jars and bottles filled with herbs and flowers while pots and pans hung from the ceiling. There was a large fireplace surrounded by oak shelves. These shelves were also covered by small jars and pots.

It was this fire which provided the only light and the heat in the room. As she started to feel a little overcome, Agnes became aware of a very small woman seated on of the settles which were at right angles to the fireplace. She wore a red dress and her long grey hair was arranged loosely about her shoulders. Although obviously very old, she was nevertheless quite an attractive woman.

"Hello Miss. Would you like to sit by me here?" She patted the seat next to her.

Agnes looked at John who smiled and she took up the offer. It was strange how comfortable she felt sitting next to this woman.

"It is very kind of you to let us into your home. Do you have many visitors?" Agnes said as she removed her gloves.

"I have all the visitors I am meant to," the woman answered, still smiling.

"Oh I see." Although Agnes didn't see at all.

"Take some of the cakes from the oven Sir and then pour us all something to drink. You will find some lovely wine in the jug on the table. Go on, don't be shy."

John did as he was bid and brought over the refreshments to the women. They both felt surprisingly happy and at home in the cottage and found that they could not stop smiling.

"Now then, you two young people, shall I read your fortunes?"

"Oh, yes please!" said Agnes with rather more enthusiasm than she might have done when more guarded.

"I wouldn't mind," said John.

The old woman got up from her chair and made some room on the table. She asked John to pass her a large box from its place on a shelf by the fire place. He was obedient to the request and upon receipt she opened the box and took out some cards and placed them on a table.

They both moved over to the table while pulling up stools and Agnes took the hand painted cards and shuffled them as requested. The old lady took them from her and laid them out in a pattern on the table. She asked John to give her a ring he wore and she held this as she spoke to them.

"Now my dears, this is very interesting, shall I tell you everything I can see here?" Her accent was as broad Devonian as it was possible to be.

"Yes, yes please," they answered together.

"I see marriage and children. Ten children I think. One of the boys will be well known and influential. He will advise one Queen and three Kings and will know great highs and lows in his life. You will remain rich and landed."

"Which of us are you reading for now?" asked Agnes.

"I'm reading for the two of you together. You will marry each other this year and be very happy for many years."

Agnes blushed deeply, but inside her heart was singing.

John said nothing, just stared at the cards.

"Any questions?" she said.

"That all seems very nice …" began Agnes.

The old woman turned over another card. It was of a hooded man.

"Beware the hooded man," said Agnes facetiously.

The old woman glared and said, "Indeed yes. You must protect yourself against the Devil. He walks all of our boundaries, trying to find a way in."

Agnes and John looked at each other and grinned.

The old woman did not grin.

"I have a gentleman with me. He has the same name as you Sir."

"I don't see him," said John, suddenly nervous.

"That's because he is not alive. I believe him to be your father. Yes, he is your father. He said to tell you that he has seen King Henry again and is laughing. He had quite an adventure at Harford Church one night. The moor is full of surprises and mysterious places."

"Yes, he told me lots about his adventures and took me on some. Errr – is he alright?"

"He is very happy and is with his father and the rest of the clan. Apparently they travel to France and Spain and Syria, so he tells me."

"He always wanted to travel," said John uncertainly.

"I am sorry John. I didn't know that your father had passed. Was it recent?" asked Agnes.

"This summer Miss Williams, I miss him very much."

"He tells me that you shouldn't miss him too much John. He will see you eventually and you don't want to die too soon," said the old woman.

"I suppose not, although I would love to see him again. We didn't say goodbye because I was in Fowey when he died," said John.

"What would you be willing to do to see him again?"

John was taken aback with the question and answered, "I'm not sure but nothing against God!"

The woman laughed and Agnes said, "What are you saying? Is there a way he can see his father?"

The woman laid out the cards and they looked at a picture of the Devil and a bearded King.

"What does that mean?" asked Agnes.

"Do you have any gold with you?"

"Well yes, I do. Do I have to pay to see my father?"

"It will help the connection," the old woman intimated.

Agnes imagined this to be a confidence trick of some sort but John looked more hopeful. He handed over two gold sovereigns and the old woman grabbed them and put them – somewhere. She stared at the two young people, who stared back. Outside it was becoming dark and there was a rumbling across the moor.

"A storm is coming. We should go home John, the horses will spook," Agnes said, shivering.

John rose from his chair and took her hand.

"Yes, we should. I don't want to be in trouble with Great Aunt Alice or Aunt Emlyn for that matter."

They laughed.

"John." A voice neither of them recognised was calling his name.

They both turned to the old woman and were shocked to see that she was no longer sitting at the table. Instead there was a tall man dressed in a shroud standing next to the fire. He had a greenish white face, so thin it was almost skull like. He had grey hair pasted down on his head and a glow around his person which was separate to the firelight.

"Father?" asked John in a tremulous voice.

"Are you a ghost?" asked Agnes in a less anxious tone. She had been raised in a house where disembodied voices and misty figures were common during the night.

"John," said the ghoul.

Agnes walked towards the mirage and reached out to touch him.

"Don't Agnes!" shouted John. "You might make him vanish!"

Agnes withdrew her hand and the spirit, for that is what it was, walked towards them. Or perhaps it was more of a glide as its movement caused John and Agnes to move backwards.

"John," said the spirit.

"Where is the old woman?" whispered Agnes.

"She has vanished; perhaps she has left us alone here?"

"Perhaps she was dressed herself as your father's ghost in order to warrant the two gold pieces," said Agnes and giggled.

John looked at her as if the idea had only just occurred to him too and their eyes locked.

"John!" roared the spirit.

They jumped and Agnes squealed, for the spirit was now standing next to them and the smell and freezing temperature they were experiencing was paralysing them.

"What do you want spirit?" asked Agnes, for now she knew it to be so.

"John!" it repeated.

"Are you really the spirit of my father?"

"Yes!" it shouted.

"Why must you shout so?" asked Agnes. "If you speak quietly, then we can understand you just the same."

The spirit looked at her and nodded gently.

"I am happy John. Death is not a doorway which cannot be crossed both ways. There are many such doorways on Dartmoor and elsewhere."

"I don't want to go through any doorways just yet father. I have things to do here."

"Good. Then you must cheer up and get on with those things."

"What's being dead like?" asked Agnes with genuine interest.

"It's better than being here and alive. I don't like being back in this painful body."

"Why have you come back then? For the money?"

The spirit looked confused – a state surprisingly easy to recognise.

"No girl. My son here has responsibilities and I have returned to remind him that he must take on those responsibilities. I can't do it and too many people depend upon him. So get married John and get working."

"Father, I am not ready for marriage. Why do I need to become responsible when I am so young?

The spirit opened his mouth wider and wider and leant towards the couple as he roared his answer. The room vibrated and the noise and smell became overpowering and Agnes was near to tears.

"Our tenants and their families!"

The spirit appeared spent by this effort and shrank away from them and back towards the fire.

"Look after them all John, they cannot manage without your help."

He looked as small and vulnerable and sad now as John had seen him in the weeks prior to his death.

"I will father. I want you to be proud of me."

The spirit began to dissolve and with another flash of lightning was gone. The atmosphere in the room was heavy and musty and the young couple felt weak and light headed. A voice from the doorway said,

"That was worth the money Sir. I expect you are pleased with that."

"Yes, I expect I am. I'm not sure if I believe what just happened. Was that really my father's spirit?"

"Did it look like him? Did it sound like him? Did he know you?"

"All of that. I just didn't expect to see him. I didn't expect to see a ghost."

"And yet, see a ghost is what you did," she answered.

The lady took up her cards and put them back in the box and returned the ring to John, folding it into the palm of his hand.

"You are a special person Sir, don't throw that away easily."

"I won't," he said.

She went back to her chair by the fire, looking now quite old and tired.

"What do I owe you for the food and the advice?" asked John.

"Nothing Sir, nothing, I am happy to help. This is not the only time we shall meet."

Agnes nodded to him and he put two pennies onto the table. They left after saying their goodbyes and thanking her, but she appeared to have gone to sleep and did not respond.

"Come on John," said Agnes and they went out into the sunlight. It seemed very strange to be outside again, as though they had been in the cottage for hours.

"The sun has got quite low," John said. "We should be getting back."

They climbed onto their horses and rode back the way they had arrived. There was no sign of the maid and Agnes felt a stab of guilt knowing that Mary would have been very bored and probably hungry and thirsty while covering for her mistress.

"What do you think about that episode John?"

He was quiet for a moment, but it was a comfortable silence as they both now felt connected to each other.

"I think we shall get married," he said and looked at Agnes.

She smiled back at him and answered, "I think you are right. The life she promised seems too good to miss." They stopped their horses in a woodland glade and leant across to each other and kissed.

Now that felt very nice, thought Agnes. Creating ten children with this man did not seem like a problem at all.

"Grrrrr."

"Oh my Lord!" exclaimed Agnes in genuine surprise. Standing in front of them was the wolf from earlier. It was a huge beast with lips curled up over his teeth.

"Stay perfectly still," said John in the time honoured way a man feels he must deal with a dangerous situation, as he began to draw his sword.

The wolf took two steps towards them and placed his nose on Agnes's dress.

"It's alright John, he is friendly," she said and bent to stroke the wolf on his neck.

The wolf nuzzled her hand and opened his mouth. John Prideaux took his sword and jumped from his horse. Neither horse appeared perturbed by the wolf's presence.

The wolf dropped something into Agnes's hand, nuzzled her again before turning and loping away.

"Are you alright Agnes?"

"Of course I am. But look what he gave me!" She opened her small hand to reveal two gold pieces. The very coins John had given the old woman before the spirit appeared. Agnes handed them to John who took them and folded them into his hand.

"I shall have them made into our wedding rings," he said.

When they arrived back at Stowford they discovered Mary had spent the day soaking her feet in a stream and sleeping. There was much clucking and feigned disapproval from the Aunts Alice and Emlyn when they returned to the Hall.

"I humbly beg your pardon for keeping your niece out so long ladies. However, during today we have come to an understanding and I should like to marry her."

Agnes smiled at her aunt, who said,

"Well done, you are happy Agnes?"

"Yes Aunt."

"Clever girl Agnes, clever girl."

*

The couple were to live at the Prideaux family house now that both John's parents were dead.

This Prideaux property at Stowford was a beautiful estate with cottages for workers, stables and land running down to the Kings Highway. There were tracks leading directly onto the moor and John and Agnes and their planned children would make these moors their second home. The woodland groves and mock temples in the style of the Phoenicians who were said to have dwelt there at one point and the manicured Tudor gardens were the envy of the neighbourhood.

The wedding was arranged at the little church at Harford where the Prideaux and Williams families had always worshipped their God. As Agnes arrived for her wedding in a carriage from her uncle's house, she breathed in the beautiful day. The carriage and horses had been trimmed with flowers and ribbons and she knew that the church would be bedecked in a similar manner. The progress of the wedding procession was slow as the very narrow roads with high hedges made it difficult for the small carriage to travel without hitting the sides. Luckily the weather was dry and so although the rutted road was hard going for the horses, there was no mud in which the carriage wheels could come to grief. Many had used sedan chairs in the past, which progressed much more easily but Agnes wanted a fashionable arrival.

Walking in front and dressed in Sunday clothes, were the tenants and locals. Children giggled and threw flowers at Agnes and she tried to catch them. She stood up to reach a particularly lovely bunch of cornflowers and looked across the fields as she did so. She noticed a dark figure standing at the tree line. It was hooded and caped and stood motionless. Agnes felt as though time was standing still and everyone faded into a fuzzy background as the hooded man held her focus.

"Miss! Miss!" shouted one of the girls as she threw more flowers. Agnes looked round and caught the lilies.

"Thank you Hannah," she answered. Agnes added the lilies to her bouquet on the seat and she looked back to the tree line.

The figure had gone and before Agnes could consider the conundrum any further, they had arrived at Harford Church. The sight of flowers covering the gate and her family waiting and waving to her made her cry.

She alighted from the steps onto the pathway leading to the church door and took hold of her father's arm.

"You really do look lovely Agnes," he told her with pride evidenced on his large face.

"I know!" she answered and they both laughed at her modesty.

John was shuffling from foot to foot inside the church. Rector John Priest stood by the altar, alternately looking between the soon to be husband and the door. John had two of his good friends with him, John Williams and Giles Fox. They were telling him jokes about Agnes not turning up and him having to do a walk of shame back to his horse. He joined in but was feeling a little worried that she might. He went into his mind in order to quell panic.

He had begun seeing the figure shortly after the visit to the moor and the phantom visitation from his father. The first time he saw the figure was from his bedroom window two days later. The man, he firmly believed him to be such, wore a cloak with a hood which covered his face. He just stood immobile against the stone wall surrounding the yard. When one of the men came into the yard pushing a barrow, he didn't appear to see him. When John averted his eyes back to the figure – he was gone. John thought it must have been a trick of the light.

The next time was against the trees surrounding the property and the third and fourth times against the barn. The figure appeared during the daytime, remained immobile and vanished after a while.

The fifth and sixth times he saw the figure at the far end of the stables while he was getting ready to ride out. This time he went so far as to ask the lad if he could see him and the answer was no. But the lad said that there were often strangers coming looking for food and he always sent them away.

"Unless he's a ghost," he added.

"Ghost? You see ghosts William?" asked John.

"Sometimes Sir. Ghosts from the past and from the moor. Everyone does, do you?"

"Not sure William. Perhaps."

This continued over the weeks leading to the wedding. John told no one, because he didn't want to be thought of as deranged. He put it down to his anxieties following his father's death and the further responsibilities which were coming his way.

Then only a week ago, he had been in the house on his own. That was highly unusual, because even when the family was away, there were servants around. But this day was different. His sister and cousins were away in Cornwall and one of the maids was marrying the stonemason. John had attended the ceremony at Harford as was his duty as landowner and he had given the servants time off until midnight. He had supplied food and drinks for the tenants and then returned to the house in order that they may enjoy themselves without the Master present.

He realised shortly after his arrival back at Stowford House that it was the first time he had been there alone. He wasn't sure that he liked it very much. He went inside and quickly bolted the door behind him. He didn't really know why. Then, even though this made him feel a little stupid he still walked slowly around the ground floor, fastening windows and battening doors. He wanted the house safe by the time it got dark.

John went into the kitchen and poured some wine into a goblet favoured by his father. The container gave him comfort and lately he had been holding it more tightly than usual. What the hell had that been at the witch's house? Was it his father? It certainly seemed so, but he had also been soooo – odd. Perhaps that was what death did to you.

There was a noise upstairs and John froze, with the goblet to his lips. He listened with everything he had and heard it again. Footsteps and yes, something being knocked over.  He put down the wine and moved stealthily towards the hallway. He wasn't breathing and so had to begin with tiny breaths in order that he didn't faint. He felt a nudge on his leg and almost screamed. Looking round he saw his dogs, two small terriers, mother and daughter. They were scratching his leg and begging to be picked up. This he did, for he could hear the noises upstairs again.

He made sure that his dagger was at his belt and crept towards the stairs. He ought to shout and see who was there, but somehow he couldn't. The dogs would generally wiggle in his arms, but this evening they were not. They were calm, almost subdued. John hoped they weren't getting ill, he couldn't stand losing these dogs. They were like his children.

John stood on the bottom step, looking up. He could see the stained glass window at the head of the stairs and the small landing there, where the stairs split again left and right. He couldn't see around there - obviously. He was wondering whether to go up and look when a noise from behind him made his body shoot fear through his soul. He turned around slowly, so very slowly and saw what he dreaded. The hooded man was standing in the hall, backed against the front door. The head was lowered so that the hood hid his face, showing only a dark shadow.

John didn't think he had ever been so scared. His dogs whimpered and John's thoughts went directly to protecting them.

"Who are you?" he asked.

There was no answer, apparently not all ghosts speak.

"Why are you doing this? I'm not afraid of you."

The hooded head began to rise, revealing more of the dark shadow space beneath. The creature began to move quietly across the stone floor towards John.

"Stop!" shouted John.

It didn't. It walked slowly and appeared to cover more ground than if he had run. John should move or the creature would be in front of him soon - too soon. His dogs barked and John thawed and turned to run up the stairs. At the small landing he went left and ran again. He was aware that he seemed to be losing his strength and so tried to breathe deeper. He felt like an old man as he tried to get some distance between that thing and him. Although John refused to look, it never seemed to be too far behind him and John was trying to think where he could hide.

It was pointless going into a bedroom he thought. He must go to the attic and reach the hidden room at the far end. The feeling of fear in his middle and around his heart was stifling and he guessed that today was the day he would die. Dying could not feel any worse than this. This must be a heart attack or a brain explosion. John kept hold of the dogs as he scrabbled through the attic door. He shut the door behind him and locked it and he put the dogs on the floor.

John and his two best dogs ran up the attic steps and already he could hear the thing banging against the door, trying to get to them. The dogs were one with him now and he whispered,

"Puppies, puppies - come on girls. Come with me. We must hide." He must protect them at all costs. Their lives and safety seemed more important than his own, especially if he was to die right here, right now. He couldn't leave them to the mercy of this monster.

He moved some cabinets and opened the supposedly invisible door in the wall where John scooched the dogs in and he followed quickly. As he closed the door and barred it, he heard the attic door at the stair bottom give way. He thought he would cry. He put his fingers to his lips and said,

"Ssssh my little babies. Don't make any noise, we don't want him to hear us." The dogs understood him and hid under a small bed in the corner. John moved some small boxes in front of their hidey hole.

"There girls, you are safe so long as you don't make a noise and show your faces. Please, please, please stay safe."

John turned and heard the thing banging against his door. Then the wood began to crack and splinter and John saw a hand peep through the ragged hole. The leather gloved fingers broke the wood until the demon's hooded face could fit through. Now John could see the dark skeletal face and hollow eyes staring at him. There was no noise coming from it, not even as it smashed the door down.

"Why are you doing this? Are you the Devil? Please stop!"

The head was pushing through now and the demon's shoulders were showing. John felt inside his shirt and pulled out the crucifix given to him by his mother. He thrust it into the face of this devil man. The action achieved nothing.

"Please," said John- he had never felt so weak in his life. He thrust the crucifix wildly from side to side, trying to touch the thing in its face and – stop it somehow. The fear in his soul that he didn't think could get any worse – was getting infinitely worse. He was going to die, he knew that he was dying right there and then as he felt his heart cease and the blood stop circulating. The fear was leaving him, he was moving away and he heard a voice saying,

"John. Stop it. Stop the world."

It was his father. John slumped back against the bed and reached under it for his dogs.

"The world has stopped John. Your world has stopped. Look around you."

John did look. The demon had stopped - its face and hood and shoulders half in, half out of the broken door. It appeared dead. John looked under the bed and the puppies were snuggled together and he touched them. His hand went through their bodies. His father pointed to the round attic window and John looked outside. He saw the scene he recognised, the horses in the field and the farm and the trees. Everything had stopped and it was as a painting, flatly spread out in front of him.

"Am I dead, Father?" he asked.

His father laughed and John awaited his fate.

"We are all dead, my son."

"Did I have a heart attack? Was it my brain? What happens now? Do I get to see Jesus?"

"No John. We are all alive and dead at the same time."

"I don't understand."

"See all of this? Everything is flat, lifeless. Can you see?"

"I thought that was because I was dead? I am talking to you, that's proof enough I should say."

"You are recognising that we create our life. We can start it and stop it if we don't like it."

"I still don't understand."

"You saw that demon following you. You created it. It is there because you are full of fears and anxieties and you think they are closing in on you. You try and run away from them and they keep coming and then you fight them and they are still there."

"I don't see, Father."

"You have just stopped your unpleasant creation. Now you can see that it isn't as real as you believe it to be. Nothing is as real as you think it is. You give it life with your thoughts and you can take its life away."

"What should I do now?"

"For a start I should get rid of that demon there and have something much nicer. A happy life, a happy marriage, anything you want."

"And where will the demon go? Will he be hiding back in the house?"

"He only exists because you allow him to. Decide you don't want it in your life. Decide what you want in your life."

"But, the Devil?"

"The Devil only exists when you recognise him. So don't. The Devil is only doubt personified. Ignore him as you would ignore a person you no longer want to have contact with. Pay him no attention. Trust in yourself."

"Alright Father."

John felt the tension leave him and his fear went the same way. His shoulders dropped and he saw that he was in control. The demon vanished, the door fixed and his dogs yapped and scrabbled at the boxes in front of the bed. John moved them and the dogs ran to him and sat wagging on his lap, licking and nuzzling him.

"If you want to keep the Devil away, then only imagine the things you want. Don't give him the chance to sneak back into your life."

"Should I go to church more?" asked John, who was not a big churchgoer.

"Not necessarily, nor try and be really good. Just be aware that you are going to get what you think and the Devil is part of that."

"Are you sure about this? And are you really my father?"

"I am."

The spirit disappeared.

John went downstairs and the dogs happily followed him as if nothing had happened. He felt nothing out of the ordinary. He felt no fear that a demon would appear because he saw that he was causing it to come.

As he took some bread and meat, throwing some down to the dogs and thought about what had just happened, he felt light hearted and somehow free. He thought about his estate and his dogs and Agnes and how life without any of them would be unbearable. Then he stopped.

"I should be careful how I think," he said to his dogs.

He had been fine and managed to correct his wayward fears until just now at the church. The old feelings of, 'what if this was the wrong thing to do' and 'this marriage with Agnes is until I die.' He stopped his world and readjusted his thoughts. He wasn't sure how his thoughts affected other people and he didn't want Agnes scared or hurt. He didn't want to project his fears and his monsters on to her.

John smiled as broadly as any man could do when he saw his bride walking towards him. He reminded her on many occasions during their life together, of how he felt at that moment. Telling her about it meant he could calm her down when she was worried or upset and cheer her up when she was cross with him.

The witch on the moor was right - they were meant for each other.

"We are meant for each other," said Agnes.

"What is that my dear?"

Agnes opened her eyes and saw a woman in a cap looking at her and smiling.

"What are you saying my dear? Do you need a drink or something?"

"No, I don't. Where is my family? Where are my girls and my boys?"

"Thomas and Blanche are coming this afternoon and John will be here later."

"Good. I won't be around for much longer so I need to see them all during this week."

"Now we don't want any talk like that. You are just being a silly girl."

"Don't talk to me as though I am an idiot, my mind is perfectly sharp, I have decided to join my husband in Heaven. He is expecting me."

"That's right my dear, whatever you say. I shall just go and organise your lunch."

The nurse scuttled out of the room and Agnes sat herself up in bed. Although she was determined to die as soon as she had sorted out her estate, she was not as ill as she let the others believe. Agnes was quite sure that she would be dying this summer and that was fine.

She thought of the witch on the moors.

Everything she said had come true. Neither she nor John had ever told anyone else that they consulted Grace Trelawney on many occasions and her advice had always been good. She had finally died at well over 100 years old many years ago after telling Agnes that she would see them both soon. Each time she saw the hooded figure, she would speak to John. He told her that the rings would keep them safe,

"We must never take off the rings," he told her.

Her beloved John died peacefully on the second day of the New Year 1616 and devastated Agnes. The weather had been freezing cold. Snow began to fall during the middle of December 1615 and had continued through to March 1616. It meant that the grave they dug for John had taken days because the ground was too solid.

The funeral had to be held up until the work was finished. The children kept trying to tell their mother that the delay was caused by something else as they did not want to upset her. Agnes was seeing the hooded figure almost all of the time and she would close her eyes tightly, praying to John to come and save her. Every time she opened her eyes he was gone again.

"Don't be silly my children, this is not the first year that it has taken a long time to dig a grave. I expect your father does not want to go into the ground before me."

"Mother, please don't say such things, it scares me!" said Johan.

"Your father was almost eighty years old and I am seventy. We have had our time and a very happy time it has been. I consider myself to be a very lucky woman. I have had money and happiness and best of all ten wonderful, clever, handsome children. What more could I ask for?"

"You have paid back any good fortune you have had. Father and you have been generous and kind to your family and also to your neighbours. You have been welcome in all the big houses and good families hereabouts but have never failed in your duty to those worse off. We are all very proud of you both," said Thomas, her eldest son. He was to inherit the entire properties and estate but Agnes knew he would look after his brothers and sisters.

Once her husband was buried, Agnes retired to Churchland at the corner of the lands which overlooked the Ivy Bridge. Previously there had been an alehouse and prior to that a chapel on this spot. The older buildings were now incorporated in the outhouses. She took two maids with her whom she knew would look after her every need.

Thomas sent a man down most days to deal with any heavy or outside work. Agnes walked over to the main house most days and supervised work being done there too, much to the indignation of Blanche, Thomas's wife but who wisely kept her tongue.

Agnes rang the bell which had been left on her night table for that very purpose. After a few seconds the maid came into the room.

"Yes Mrs. Prideaux, what can I do for you?"

"Inform my children that we shall be having a picnic on the moor this Sunday. They must all attend and you must organize all the food and drink. We shall go by Harford Church on the way and attend service together. See to it Mary."

The maid looked at her mistress and guessed what was on her mind. She had seen this before - gathering the family together and setting everything to rights.

The end was near.

Mary smiled and said, "Of course Mrs. Prideaux, consider it done. You shall have a great day, the best day of your life."

"Not the best, Mary. That was the day I married my John."

On the following Sunday a long line of Prideauxs riding in traps and riding horses, set off early towards Harford Church. Rector Andrew Helyer watched them all arrive from the church door. He had been forewarned about the event and he wanted to ensure that his great benefactor Agnes Prideaux was looked after properly. He made sure that her pew had a blanket upon it. The church was incredibly damp and many parishioners believed that bad chests were inevitable if the parson preached for too long.

Agnes was dressed in a beautiful gown of pale blue and white. Her husband loved her in these colours, they suited her so well.

Her hair still lustrous and shiny although now grey was styled carefully. Agnes had no need of a wig and as she stepped down from the carriage, was still a head turner. The family bustled around her and walked slowly with her up the path to the church.

They walked the very same steps to the church door that she had walked thousands of times before. The trees swayed in the light breeze and the flowers on the grassy banks and around the graveyard, dazzled the eye and threw out their scent in the glorious early sunshine. The old stone cross by the gate was covered with lilies and cornflowers on the instruction of her son Thomas.

"Good morning Mrs. Prideaux. It is an absolute pleasure to see you looking so well. I have heard such bad news about your health of late."

"I shall call you to the house when I am ready to go, have no fear. But today I am enjoying a day out with my family."

"It is wonderful to see all your children and grandchildren with you. There will be some squashing to fit them all in today."

Agnes glided into the church followed by her family. The local people, who turned out in numbers this morning were rewarded with a great spectacle of Prideaux finery.

"I would rather they all gathered for me while I lived than after my death," she whispered to Thomas.

"You are very naughty, mother," was his answer.

Later that morning, the party made their way up to the moor and the women set out chairs and the picnic.

"There is so much food here Blanche, I wonder whether it will all be eaten."

"Never fear mother, we shall eat all of this before we return. The men and the children are always hungry!"

A canopy was raised over the chair and table which Agnes was to use. Other canopies were placed round the same area and soon the whole area looked very promising.

"This is beautiful," said Agnes. "But this is not as sparse as when your father and I used to come here on our own. We only brought a little food and drank water from the stream. But I have to say that the water did not taste as nice as this wine. I do miss John and coming to see the old lady in the cottage."

Agnes smiled as she began to nod off.

The rest of the Prideaux clan watched her carefully and the hearts of her children were collectively filled with a mixture of love and nostalgia. They knew instinctively that Agnes was not long for this world, even though she could quite easily live another ten years if she put her mind to it. But it was not to be, for Agnes was determined to join her husband.

"He will be lonely without me," she said, whenever asked why.

Birds circled overhead and every so often a rabbit or a wild cat could be seen. The grandchildren enjoyed pointing out any wildlife and having it identified by the adults. The Prideauxs encouraged education at every opportunity and they expected their offspring to know the names of all flora and fauna and learn about the history of Devon and Cornwall, in addition to their own family history.

Agnes opened her eyes and watched her large brood playing and resting in the sun. Some sat in chairs under canopies and some lay flat on their backs enjoying the sun on their faces.

Her eyes wandered over to the line of ancient stones to her right. John and she had spent many hours around these old monuments and if she were to tell the truth to her families, four of them had been conceived there.

There it was - the lone wolf. He looked over at the group and then fixed Agnes with a stare of recognition. Agnes laughed and shouted,

"Hello John!"

The wolf stayed for a few minutes and then turned away from the stones and vanished.

"Time to head for home now, mother," said Francis. Henry followed his brother as he always did. Henry her fourth child had a learning difficulty, but was clever nonetheless.

"Mother when you die, you will be living here won't you?"

"Yes Henry, I shall be here with your father."

"I shall visit you here when I want to speak to you then."

They hugged.

Soon everyone was loaded back onto the traps and making their way down from the moors. Agnes was happy and tired in equal measure. The sun was now low in the sky but still radiated heat and light which made their journey a very pleasant one. The further down the valley they travelled, the more flies, bees and butterflies came to join them. Agnes listened to the birdsong and watched the wildflowers waving in the light breeze. By the time they arrived back at the large house she had known from being a young girl, she felt about 20 years old.

Agnes was so relaxed that her sons were able to carry her carefully into her bedroom.   After being undressed by her maids, she asked that they bring her children into her room.

As they were all assembled Agnes said,

"I want you all to know that I love you all equally and I have enjoyed my life with you and particularly today, more than I can ever say. I must leave the property to Thomas as that is the way things are done. However, the rest of you have either made good marriages or have enough money of your own."

"Mother, why are you talking like this? It is upsetting me," said Richard.

"Because she wants everything sorted out so that she can fly with the birds tomorrow," explained Henry.

"That is correct, Henry. I just want you to know that you must enjoy and make the best of every moment of your life, because our life here is very short. I heard that time and time again from my elders and I thought that they were just jealous because I was younger and they had made a mess of their own lives. There are the early days when you are feeling superior because of your youth and then, when not expecting it, someone tells you that you are too old to understand and you cannot work out what day everything changed. So, goodnight all and God bless."

The family trooped out of her room and when they sat downstairs a little later on, the mood was sombre. The women still wore their finery from their day out and the men were tanned and glowing from the sun. All the children were now in bed back at the main house in the care of the maids.

"I hope Mother is alright," said Thomas.

"She will do as she pleases, as always," said Blanche.

The nurse discovered Agnes had died in her sleep when she went to draw the curtains the following morning. She reached to close the curtains of the room in preparation for laying out the little body of her mistress. The room felt full of people, although they were the only two present. The nurse ignored this familiar feeling which she experienced every time she dealt with the recently passed.

"She looked so peaceful and happy," she commented later.

The funeral was held at Harford Church and Agnes was buried next to her beloved husband for eternity. It was only Thomas who saw two hooded black shapes standing behind the altar. He thought they were moving towards the coffin and stood up with a scream frozen in his mouth, pointing. He was pulled back down to the pew by Blanche, who imagined that he had some sort of funny turn with the stress of it all.

When Thomas and Henry were riding out on the moor a week later, they travelled to their last picnic place. As they rested for a moment and remembered quietly that last Sunday, Henry spoke,

"Look over there Thomas! Mother and Father together again!"

Thomas looked in the direction Henry pointed, but all he could see were a pair of wolves standing together by the ancient stones. The four of them looked at each other for a time before the wolves turned and walked off to be lost in the mists of the moor. Thomas reached for the two rings he had hanging from a leather thong around his neck. The ones their parents had worn. Thomas had taken the rings from their parents' bodies.

Thomas never told anyone in the family that he had taken them. He also didn't know how much he was now protected.

"Wolves mate for life you know, Thomas," said Henry. "Just like our Mother and Father."

## STOWFORD DEMONS

### featuring Thomas and Blanche Prideaux of Stowford

**1588**

"Oh Mother! It was so exciting! I have definitely decided that I want to be a sailor!"

Thomas Prideaux was sixteen years old and full of wonder and awe ever since he had accompanied his father to Plymouth and seen the might of the English Navy docked there and awaiting a battle with the Spanish Armada.

"There were hundreds of ships in the harbour and sailors all over the town. They are waiting for the Spanish fleet."

"That sounds a little worrying," said his mother. These skirmishes had been going on for years now and Agnes was scared that one day these dreadful foreign people would land at Plymouth and invade their county.

As if reading her thoughts, Thomas continued,

"There is talk that the Spanish are coming to invade England via Plymouth. They say that they will land there and march through the countryside towards London and kill the Queen."

"Don't frighten your brothers and sisters with talk like that, Thomas," warned his father John.

"But your cousin Captain Prideaux is sailing with the fleet and he told me what was happening. He would not lie to me would he?"

"It is not a question of lying - it is a matter of what we talk about in front of the family," said his father carefully.

"What is happening John? This talk worries me," said Agnes.

"I will tell you later, there is nothing to worry about. The Navy is sorting out the problem."

The children carried on with their meal. In other large houses such as theirs, the children would generally eat with the maids but not in this Prideaux household. The whole family sat down and ate their meals together. This ensured that the family was not only close but also that there were very few secrets to be kept.

Thomas, Johan, Agnes, Henry, John, Hugh, Christopher, Richard, Elizabeth and Francis sat around the large oak table on chairs of varying heights, while their parents John and Agnes sat at either end of the table. The family lived in a large granite house and farmed land in Stowford. They were great friends with the Williams family, their nearest neighbours.

The Williams' ancestors along with the inhabitants of Harford and Cornwood looked to the moor for their income through tin mining and farming. John's Great Aunt Alice Prideaux had married Adam Williams, his wife's great uncle and the families remained connected through blood lines and friendship.

Food was passed down the table and Agnes continued her lecture.

"Our Queen will have the whole situation in hand. She knows better than any of the men under her control about Philip and the Spanish threat. She is the greatest monarch this country has ever known and I am convinced that so long as she draws breath, there will never be another invasion on the shores of England. So do not be concerned my children. We are safe."

John gave a round of applause.

"Well said my love, although I am sure that Philip would be less content to invade us if privateers from this country did not constantly steal from his ships!"

"They are only getting back that which is rightfully ours." Agnes could always be relied upon to stand up for a woman. She taught her children the same beliefs and her husband John, a man with great regard and respect for his own mother would never try and alter those teachings.

"Anyway the beacons worked well and the Fleet knew when the Armada appeared off St Michaels Mount in Cornwall."

"How did they do that?" asked young John, always a questioning child. At nine years old he told anyone who would listen, that he intended to make his way in the larger world. His family was quite used to his questioning attitude and his mother encouraged him whenever she could.

"Because a fire is kept ready to light on all high places along a chain from Lands End to London and beyond. As soon as those Devil ships were sighted off Cornwall, the first fire was lit and as soon as that fire was seen by the people manning the next one, then that fire was lit," answered Thomas, always happy to show that he knew more than his younger siblings.

"I hear that Prideaux Castle was one of the beacons."

"You are right about that Mother," said Thomas.

"The Navy left Plymouth and chased the Spanish up the Channel. Mark my words, our Queen will have them defeated before the end of the month," announced Father.

"Let us raise our glasses to our great and glorious Queen Elizabeth!" said Agnes and all at the table obeyed, with the exception of the babies who merely laughed and banged spoons at the general merriment.

The children worked around the farm as soon as they were old enough, but their parents also insisted they attended their education and in addition a local and retired Oxford man taught them. Their education added to the great confidence of a wealthy family. Harford Church was attended every Sunday, as religion featured strongly in the lives of the Prideauxs.

"It does not do any harm for our neighbours to see us attend church and show them our finery on a Sunday," said Agnes many times. To be truthful, Agnes and John felt very strongly about their connections to the Williams and other more affluent branches of the Prideaux family and enjoyed the social extension which church attendance offered. On more than one occasion a financial contribution had been made when pressed by the Rector. John had inherited all the properties and lands they occupied just before he married Agnes. They were responsible for tenants and house and farm servants. However the cash flowed less easily while their glorious Queen fought her expensive political battles and so stretched her tax hikes as far as Devon and Cornwall.

In spite of all this, the couple ensured that all of their sons attended the Ashburton Grammar School. Thomas was always going to inherit the Stowford farm, but John and Agnes intended that the rest of the family should be set up in good careers or trades.

**1594**

John was proving to possess the greatest academic gifts and he applied for the post of parish clerk at Ugborough parish church when he was sixteen and due to leave the grammar school.

He attended an interview and although failed to obtain the post, Lady Fowell, yet another well connected cousin, heard him sing a psalm so beautifully that she immediately insisted that he attend further education at Ashburton under a scholarship from her in order to learn more Latin. John was ecstatic and his parents overjoyed. Thomas and the others were less interested in their brother's apparent good luck. They instead chose to dwell on the interview where there had been a singing competition between John and another in front of the entire congregation at Ugborough after the morning service. They listened to both singers and decided that the other boy was the best and therefore, apparently, a better bet for the role of parish clerk. There were many times in later years when John would call in at the church on his visits home in his envious finery, just to say hello.

"What are you going to do with all this learning John?" asked Henry.

"Go to London and meet the Queen," was his answer.

"Will you tell her about me, John?"

"Of course."

"What shall you tell her?"

"What a clever brother I have who is always kind to animals and can charm the wild creatures right out of their holes and onto his knee."

Henry laughed. It was of little concern to Henry that he was not quite as quick in the mind as the others and that schooling had been out of the question for him. He was happy exactly as he was and no one would argue with that.

Hugh was a boy full of mischief and devilment. He would hide when everyone else was ready for church and would only appear as the two carriages began to leave the drive ready to make the journey through the narrow lanes towards Harford.

One Sunday on the return journey he incurred the wrath of his elder brother Thomas.

"Tom has got a girlfriend! Tom has got a girlfriend!" Hugh had shouted over and over again. Thomas leant over and caught Hugh a good thump across the head.

"Thomas! What has got into you?"

"Nothing Mother," he answered.

"Then apologise to your brother. This is the Lord's day."

"I am sorry Hugh," Thomas said dutifully but insincerely. His eyes told Hugh that as soon as they were out of sight of their parents, he would clout him again.

Thomas had not had a good weekend. He was in love, madly in love with Blanche, the daughter of another gentleman farmer and who lived near Cornwood. Blanche loved Thomas too, but marriage was out of the question.

Blanche told anyone who enquired that her father needed her at home to keep him company now that her mother was dead. Because of his frail health he would not countenance her marrying anyone. Blanche was a more than a little frightened of her father she said and felt duty bound to stay with him. Unfortunately her mother had made her promise to look after her father and be obedient to him, while on her deathbed.

"Deathbed requests are not fair," reasoned Thomas. "After all, we change our minds constantly and to have something we said once apply forever, just does not make any sense. Your mother would want you to be happy and I will make you happy."

"Don't say that Thomas. I did promise Mother and perhaps as more time passes, Father will come round and we can marry."

"But you won't even let me ask him!"

"I don't want him upset. Things will work out for the best, you see."

"Well perhaps I don't want to wait until things work out Blanche. I can't wait around for you forever, I have needs too."

"Don't then," said Blanche and turned on her heel.

"I shall join the Navy then and you will never see me again!" he shouted at her.

"Good! Then your brother shall inherit the estates and I shall marry him instead!"

That was yesterday and Thomas had regretted what he said immediately. He watched her walk away from him and he climbed on his horse and began the ride back to Stowford. That afternoon had not gone as he planned. Then this morning at church, Blanche stayed close to her sister and did not look in his direction once. He felt terrible.

Agnes noticed all, but chose to say nothing. She would wait until she was on her own with her son and sort out his problems then. But due to their busy life, they did not have chance to talk until the following Thursday just after dinner. Agnes fulfilled her promise and told her son that she would see if she could persuade Blanche's father to accept a married daughter. Agnes liked Blanche and she wanted Thomas to be as happy as she and John had been.

"If we put our minds together, we shall work something out, you see," she told him. Thomas hugged his mother, he really loved her.

## 1596

Upon John Prideaux's successful graduation from Ashburton School, another opportunity for him came up. Lady Fowell had insisted that he should follow his fellow West Countrymen and attend Exeter College at Oxford University. She promised to sponsor him so long as he remained frugal.

John and Agnes discussed the matter at the meal table as usual. The family all listened intently.

"Oxford is a big step for any man John," his father informed him.

"I know father, but I am up to the task. I love learning and I find it easy to do. The only problems for me will be paying for the education and leaving you all in the lurch back here with regard to the farm. Lady Fowell has said she will help."

"We are coping easily with the work, John," said Thomas. "Hugh is old enough now and Richard works hard after school."

"I help too!" said Henry.

"Without your help and support, we should not be able to cope, Henry," answered his father with meaning.

"I think that you should go and make us all proud," said his mother.

"How shall I pay?" asked John. He desperately wanted to go to the great university and be one of the names who would be recorded forever. Lucky for him that Elizabethan Britain was a place where even the less well-off could be educated if they set their mind to it.

"We shall speak to our cousins and see what can be arranged," said Agnes, determined that her son should be an Oxford man. That would be something to boast about.

It was soon settled. Money was collected and put to one side for John's education. John decided that he would make his own way to Oxford and save money. Cousins from Devon would be awaiting his arrival and a job working in the kitchens at Exeter College had been arranged. He was to wait on as a servitor on his fellow sojourners and the Fellows of the college. In return he would receive board and lodging and pay only a small amount for tuition.

Exeter College had been founded in 1314 by Bishop Stapledon, the same worthy man who had founded Ashburton College. Many of the great and good West Countrymen attended both institutions.

John planned to walk to Oxford from Stowford, a total of 170 miles, in a pair of leather breeches which he kept hanging in his wardrobe for the rest of his days. They helped keep his mind out of the clouds, he said.

With numerous instructions from his mother, John set off early one morning in late September 1596 in order to make the life changing journey to Oxford University. He was given a lift to the Kings Highway by Thomas and hoped to get another lift from there on one of the many carts which made their way along that road.

Agnes insisted that he should not walk from their front door to the highway which ran along the edge of their land. John pointed out that he could quickly walk over the fields, over the gate and be on the road, but she would have none of it.

"It is bad enough that you must walk from there," she said.

A debate had opened about the possibility of finding a ship from Plymouth to London, but John was not as keen on this option as he would have little control should anything go wrong.

"I wish you all the luck in the world, John. I shall miss you greatly," his big brother Thomas said to him.

"I shall miss you too, big brother. I hope you are married to that girl of yours the next time I see you."

Thomas reddened and looked at the ground.

"I shall let you know brother."

They both felt embarrassed. Years of pushing each other around and arguing had prepared them badly for this goodbye.

"Got the prayer?" asked Thomas.

"In my bag," answered John, patting the leather satchel.

"You know it by heart though."

"We all do," answered John.

With no prompting, they both chanted,

**"O God, That knowest us to bee set in the midst of so many and great dangers, that for Mans frailenesse we cannot always stand uprightly, guard to us the health of Body and Soul, that all those things which we suffer for sinne, by thy holy wee may well passé and overcome, through Jesus Christ our Lord."**

The prayer had been handed down through the Prideaux family and had been used particularly to ward off plague.

"We shall see each other many times Thomas, do not despair. I shall make my family proud."

"It does not matter. Even if you do not achieve what you set out to do, we shall always be proud of you." The brothers hugged and faced each other.

"Are you going to watch me walk away?" asked John sheepishly.

"No, ride away, here is another lift. You have your money and everything?"

"Yes Thomas, I will write to you all as soon as I am in Oxford." John leapt aboard the back of a cart, the driver of which the young men knew vaguely and John sat facing his brother and his home until they rounded the next corner.

John would never live at Stowford again.

The road was not a great deal wider than the back lanes. Only a cart and a horse could comfortably pass each other. The roads travelled up and down the hills and turned past every nook and cranny. There appeared to have been no attempt to make a straight road anywhere. It had once been said in Parliament when discussing the state of the Devonian highways, that they may as well be turned into canals, there was so much running water to be found upon them.

The day was a beautiful summer day with the green hedges and flowers reflected against the blue sky. Thomas watched until the cart rounded a corner and then he clicked at his horse and made his way back to the farm.

Thomas was surprised to realise that he was silently crying. The family was always together and now with John leaving so soon after both Johan and Agnes had announced their intentions of marrying local men - it felt as though the whole family were splitting up.

Thomas became deep in thought as he headed back to the house and then suddenly he turned the pony and trap around at the end of the lane and headed towards Cornwood.

Thomas arrived at the door of Blanche's home and knocked. A maid answered.

"Where is Miss Bigbury?" he asked.

"At the stables Sir," she answered. Her eyes were taking in the entire scene. She would have a lot to tell cook about Master Prideaux coming to the front door and looking all upset.

Thomas led his horse round to the stables and saw Blanche about to mount her horse.

"Blanche, I must talk to you!"

"Oh, Thomas, I didn't expect you. I am going riding now." Blanche's maid was also in attendance but nothing was going to stop Thomas now.

"Blanche, I want you to marry me and I don't want to wait."

"Is that so?" she answered and began to trot on.

"Blanche will you stop and listen to me?"

Blanche waited until Thomas caught up with her and asked, "Has John left now?"

"Yes he has, I have dropped him at the highway this morning. Blanche I love you and want to marry you, may I please ask your father's permission?"

Blanche was impressed with his persistence. Today she was feeling saucy and said,

"Yes Thomas, you may."

Thomas thought he would burst, but instead of doing that, he allowed Blanche to ride away, giggling with her maid.

He drove the trap directly back to the house. A sulky maid answered the door this time and glared at the trap left in front of the house,

"The Master won't like that cart being left out there."

"Have a man move it then. I doubt I shall be long."

John was eventually led into the library by the scowling maid and he prepared to wait there until Philip Bigbury should appear.

He didn't have to wait long for after a few minutes the library door began to creak open and a face peered around it. In all the nine years he had courted Blanche, he had never met her father, as he was always ill and incapacitated. So for that reason Thomas had no way of telling if the man who shuffled into the room with the aid of a heavy stick was Mr. Bigbury or not. Thomas quite naturally assumed that he was.

Thomas stood up as Bigbury came further into the room and held out his hand saying,

"It is a pleasure to meet you Sir. I am Thomas Prideaux of Stowford and I am here to ask for your daughter's hand in marriage."

Bigbury looked at him as though he were a tree talking. Thomas smiled, waiting for a response from his prospective father to be, but found it difficult to maintain when there was no response. He tried again,

"Sir, may I help you to your chair?"

As Thomas walked towards him, the man raised his stick in the air and brought it down hard on Thomas's arm. Thomas pulled it back and began rubbing it in order to ease the sting, puzzled and bemused.

"Sir, why did you do that? I have done you no harm!"

Bigbury did not answer and instead shuffled towards Thomas, waving the stick as though it was a sword and this was a battle. The stick landed heavily on Thomas's arm and it hurt. John tried to grab it but the old man hit him across the head, drawing blood. Thomas dodged past him and made for the library door. It should open easily but he still pulled the handle sharply, hoping for a quick escape and sanity returning. When this produced no positive result he knocked on the door and shouted.

"Why do you shout?" asked the old man.

"Because you keep hitting me with your stick Sir and I don't want to retaliate and make things worse."

"I will kill you," he said.

"But why Sir? Because I wish to marry your daughter? I love her and have loved her for years and if we don't marry soon I shall have to marry someone else and provide heirs for the Prideaux estates. I don't want anyone else, I want your daughter and she wants me." Thomas realised he was sounded plaintive, but his heart was racing and his anxiety levels high.

"I like killing people, I have killed before and I will kill again. I must." Bigbury's face seemed to turn into a much younger image than before and he began to move in a jerky manner towards Thomas.

Thomas, for his part was feeling hot and sweaty. No one was coming to the door in response to his cries and he was now wedged against the corner of the door jam and the wall. He became properly scared when he discovered that he was losing control of his limbs and his senses. Bigbury was close to him now, his face upturned because he was at least a foot shorter than Thomas. His old arms were surprisingly strong and they grasped John like a vice. His breath smelt and Thomas was horrified to notice the teeth on the old man. They were long and looked so sharp and his tongue was licking the air, long and red and...

When Thomas woke he noticed three people standing over him. He recognised the maid who had granted him access, a manservant of some kind and a gentleman.

"Prideaux, Prideaux, what's all this?" asked the gentleman.

"Errr, mmm. The man, the old man. He did this."

The gentleman gave instructions for Thomas to be helped to the chair because of his very wobbly legs. Wine was brought and after drinking some, Thomas felt better and able to talk.

"Bigbury, he was trying to kill me I think. I don't know why."

"Bigbury?" asked the gentleman. "I am the only Bigbury here and I found you in a dead sleep and blocking my library doorway. We had to enter through the windows from outside."

"But the old man? With the stick and the teeth and the smell?"

The others looked at each other with concern.

"Please describe him to us Prideaux," instructed the gentleman.

This Thomas did and the gentleman sat down, shoulders slumped.

"It seems you have seen our ghost, Prideaux. He hasn't been about for a while."

"Ghost? What? Who is he? He was real, not a ghost!"

"He is a ghost. He is my great uncle and he used to live in the attic because he …" began the gentleman.

"He used to attack and kill people and they kept him locked up until he died. But he missed the place and won't leave. He doesn't generally make himself visible to strangers now and I'm not really sure why he chose you."

It was Blanche saying this and she came over to Thomas, knelt next to him and stroked his face. Thomas took her hand and kissed it.

"We can marry now, father. Thomas knows the truth and won't tell anyone, will you?"

"Tell anyone? About a ghost?"

"No, about the murders," said the real Mister Bigbury.

"I didn't get from what you told me that he actually used to murder people."

"He still does," said the maid.

"Leave us Anna and fetch more wine and perhaps some food," instructed Blanche.

"This is the real reason you could not marry. We are not so shamed about having a ghost, it is the fact he is a member of our family and a killer," Bigbury whispered.

"I want to marry Blanche and therefore I shall tell no one," said Thomas.

"Alright," agreed Bigbury as he leant back heavily in his chair. "My boy, I know your family very well and your parents are people of their word. I do not have the strength to look after my daughters for all of their lives. I want them to have husbands on whom I can rely."

Bigbury appeared beaten and spent - his face now much paler than when he had entered the room. The stress of the confessions appeared to be getting the better of him. Thomas sat on the chair opposite and both men heaved their breaths until they fell asleep.

**1597**

As it turned out, the marriage could not be arranged until the following summer because Blanche wanted a large affair at Harford Church and the celebrations afterwards to be held at Stowford.

A large and well attended wedding they did have and Blanche's only disappointment was that her father was too unwell to attend. He had allowed his house servants to go to Harford Church to see their mistress marry Thomas Prideaux and return for dinner and tell him all the news. Unfortunately the servants became lost in the freedom and the merriment and forgot to go back home. It was during the early hours of the morning when many were drunkenly sleeping off their celebrations, when a rider came galloping into the Prideaux House yard.

He jumped from his horse and threw the reins at a tired looking man.

"Where is your Master?" he asked.

"I ain't got no Master," he answered back in a surly manner.

"Where is the Master of this house then? Mr. Prideaux?"

The farmhand pointed to the main door and the rider strode towards it. After some conversation with a maid he was allowed in. It took almost five minutes before shouting and screaming sounded from the upstairs windows and Thomas and his father John ran out of the front door.

Old man Bigbury was dead. An unexplained fire had begun in the library of the old house during the night and the place had swiftly burnt to the ground. A passing peddler, who had seen the fire start and reported it, had also seen an old man silhouetted against the library windows. He initially said that the man had been shouting for help but on reflection, considered that the old man was probably dancing.

"I didn't think that was possible at first," he related. "But, he seemed glad the fire was burning. It wasn't old Bigbury, it was a much older man."

"Did you recognise the man?" asked someone.

"No Sir, I never saw him before. He was still at the window when the whole place was aflame and he didn't seem bothered."

"Are you sure it wasn't Bigbury asking for help?"

"Can't have been Sir. I saw him slumped against his bedroom window at the front of the house. I saw them both at the same time."

Thomas Prideaux questioned him further about the strange old man at the library window and was aghast when he realised that the peddler was describing the spirit he had seen last year. When he told Blanche, she refused to listen and said that he shouldn't be trying to cause trouble. Her father was dead and the house razed to the ground. Now her brother would be able to build anew and have their family fortunes change.

John Prideaux, who had returned from Oxford for his brother's wedding, visited the site and performed some sort of prayer and the land was now apparently free of evil.

John had soon settled down at Oxford and wrote to his family often. He worked in the kitchens as promised and spent every spare minute studying and attending lectures. He was always to be found with a book in his hand. He spent little and impressed all with his piety and kindness. His academic dedication was surpassed by none. The family hoped that he knew what he was doing in regard to evil.

Thomas did not feel so confident.

Thomas and Blanche initially lived at Bridgend at the edge of the property and Thomas continued to assist his father run the farm. Johan and Agnes left to marry and the other children kept on with their schooling and various tasks.

Henry enjoyed every one of his days - always.

Thomas and Blanche were soon the parents to John and the busy kitchen at Prideaux House added another chair to the table on Sundays and celebration times, as each new member of the ever expanding Prideaux family arrived.

Thomas's brother Richard moved into Churchland, the house next door to Bridgend, so now both new Prideaux families could overlook the Ivy Bridge. Life was busy, but generally free from trouble and strife.

## 1615

Thomas would often see dark shapes which he would have identified as a man or a hooded demon, if he had been able to speak to a sympathetic soul. Instead he told himself that as he had only seen the shadow people from the corner of his eye, he could put it down to overwork.

Once he had been standing with his father in the Church Field, behind Churchland as they discussed the cattle and which were in calf and which should be sent to the market, when he saw the shadow against the stone wall. He gasped and stopped talking,

"What is the matter Thomas?" asked his father.

"I can see something over by the wall. Can you?"

"What can you see?"

"It is probably nothing but I thought it was an old man or – well – a monk?"

Thomas dreaded his father's ridicule and so was surprised when he answered,

"So, you can see him too?"

They sat upon the stone trough which was at the farm edge of the field and told each other of their ghostly experiences.

"It seems the whole place is haunted," noted Thomas.

"Or perhaps just the Prideaux family," answered his father.

The hooded man was standing stock still against the wall, head down and caped hands held in front, supported by a cane.

"He's back," said Thomas.

"So it would seem," acknowledged John. "I haven't seen him for a while. I wonder who he has come to fetch?"

"No one I hope," said Thomas.

"If it is me Thomas," John twirled the gold wedding ring on his finger. "I want you to take this ring before I am buried. Don't tell the others why, but it will protect you from the worst."

"What about you Father?"

"I will no longer need it. I will be living a better life, just as we all will when we leave here. More fun and less stress."

Thomas looked at his father and then turned to the hooded man, still standing guard.

"And look after your mother," added John.

He put his arm around his son and walked him towards the gate on the Highway. As they climbed it, Thomas noticed that the man had now vanished.

**1616**

The intervening year had meant a lot of changes for the family.

By 1616 Thomas and Blanche were parents to John, Hugh, Susan, Richard and Thomas. Blanche was pregnant with what was to be another son, James. Thomas and his brothers Christopher and Francis all remained at home working on the farm.

But this year was also a very sad year for the family.

Grandfather John had died in the January while there was snow on the ground and Devon was colder than it had been for many winters. He was found dead in the Church Field after apparently suffering a stroke. He had gone out after breakfast and after kissing his wife as usual. It was snowing heavily and Agnes had begged him to be careful.

"You fuss about me too much Agnes. I am well wrapped up and perfectly healthy. I shall be home for lunch, so make sure there is something hot waiting for me."

Agnes held him extra tightly today although she could not explain why.

"Hey wife. What is the matter?"

"John I love you, I want you to know that."

"And I love you too little wife. What is this?"

"I saw the wolf yesterday. He came right up to me while I was walking in the gardens talking to the Goddess and touched my hand. I had such a peculiar feeling of connection. Then he vanished and I could trace no footsteps in the snow."

"You think it is an omen?"

"Perhaps. I don't know. Just be careful."

"And you be careful my wife. But if it means that I am leaving, know that I shall wait for you every day until you come to me. Don't hurry, come when you are ready."

He kissed her again, more slowly this time, and then cupped her chin before he left the house.

When she heard the terrible news later that morning, Agnes fell to her knees and sobbed as until she lost consciousness.

Rector John returned again from Oxford for the funeral. By now he was very famous in his field. He had been finally elected Rector of Exeter College just before his 35th birthday and became Canon of Christchurch, Regius Professor of Divinity and five times Vice Chancellor of Exeter College. It was as though royalty itself had arrived in Harford when John came to take the funeral service of his father. Some in the family were trying not to resent their brother as he rolled in grandly to Stowford every time there was a family tragedy or celebration. But no one said anything to him. Agnes always made the best food for his visits and would say to the rest of the family,

"Don't touch that! It's for John when he gets here!"

Johan was in pieces and hardly able to cope after her father's death. She told the others,

"I am worried about mother. She and father were so in love that I am afraid she will not last long now. She keeps talking about father being in heaven and how she wants to be with him."

"I shall talk to her," promised John. He had brought his new wife Mary Grace to meet the family, although this was a very awkward first meeting for them all.

Nevertheless she was made welcome and the family remembered this one and only trip to her husband's birthplace fondly, for Mary never returned, dying a year after Agnes.

Once their father John was buried and things had returned to some sort of normality. Agnes's health declined considerably and she talked a lot about joining her husband in death because she missed him so much. Her sons talked to her about life and death and Agnes, promised she would do her best to stay around for a little longer.

Agnes would spend a lot of time in her garden talking to the Goddess there and feeding the wolf. The family paid little attention as they left her to her own devices and smiled when she brought in her basket of flowers and fruit. Agnes sitting in the sunshine or the snow on a bench under an archway of sweet smelling roses, meditated and mind travelled across the moor with her Goddess and wolf and John.

The Goddess was a tall stone statue of a beautiful woman. The statue had been there since before living memory and was often draped in flowers on special occasions. She was considered a good listener and some said she would impart advice. A secretly Catholic Agnes treated her like the Virgin Mary, but naturally kept that fact to herself.

**1626**

When Agnes finally left them all to begin her next journey, she was buried next to John in the churchyard where they had met, married and christened all their children and attended their weddings.

Her funeral at Harford Church was attended by so many people that some were forced to stand outside in the church yard. The weather that day was beautiful and Thomas felt surreal as he helped carry on his mother's little coffin. It was at this moment that he realised just what a tiny woman she was. She had been so strong and vital all her life and now it was as though they were carrying in a doll in a box.

Harford seemed more beautiful than ever that day. More so than the day he married his beloved Blanche at this little church sitting snugly under the trees. Surrounded by a stone wall, the lane moved past it on two sides, first coming from Stowford and then leading to Dartmoor and its ancient stones, cottages and mines. On the other side, the tiny track led to Cornwood, where the family of Blanche lived.

"I shall read the will as mother wrote it, it is fairly self-explanatory." Thomas informed them. He was standing at the head of the large oak dining table with the family seated around it. These days there were enough matching chairs for the entire family to be seated.

Rector John had managed to return for his mother's funeral and was allowed to take the service. He came alone as his wife was expecting a child and could not travel but he said he must return to Oxford almost immediately.

Thomas cleared his throat and began.

*My body to be buried in the church of Harford.*

*To the poor of Harford 2s.*

*To my son Hugh 20s.*

*To my son Richard 20s.*

*To my son Christopher 20s*

*To my son Francis 20s and my greatest brasse panne.*

*To my son Henry 50s and my next greatest brasse panne.*

*To my daughter Johan 20s.*

*To my daughter Agnesse Dow my best chest and all my lynnen.*

*To John Prediaxe his sonne my best cuppe with a silver cover,*

*To Welmont Burt my little silver cupp.*

*To little Elizabeth Mychell my great brasse crocke.*

*To all my children's children 12d each.*

*To Susan Prediaxe one ewe sheep.*

*The rest to Thomas Prediaxe my son sole executor.*

*Also I give him all my rights in Stover as appears by a lease made by Richard Williams.*

*Sign of Agnes Predyaxe*

*John Bart of Wedenbury and John Shepherd overseers*

*Witnesses John Bart and John Shepherd*

*Inventory made by Richard Prideaux and John Scobble.*

"I hope everyone is happy with the outcome," said Thomas to his wife when they were lying in bed later that night.

"It's too bad if they are not," she answered. Blanche at that moment had been planning the redecoration of Stowford. Agnes had been a wonderful woman and the two women got on well but Blanche had always been subtly discouraged from altering the place in any way.

Now almost twenty years after her marriage, Blanche was free to do anything she wanted.

It had been difficult when Agnes called every day and still acted and was treated as the lady of the house. Tomorrow Blanche intended to walk around the house and gardens and write notes about her plan. She knew that Thomas would let her carry out the changes because Thomas only ever wanted a quiet life.

"That was a mean thing to say Blanche!" Thomas said to his wife.

"I know, I am sorry I did not mean it. It is just that we are very generous and kind to the rest of the family and we don't have to be. We are like that because it is the right way to be. They all know that we will help whatever goes on."

Thomas hugged Blanche. He knew exactly what she meant. Neither of them was ignorant of their responsibilities.

The couple were proud parents and enjoyed watching their own and their extended family grow. All of Thomas's brothers and sisters had married, with the exception of Henry who spent his time at the farm but lived with Francis his younger brother whom particularly got on with him. This move happened when Francis's first wife had died in childbirth and Henry went to stay with him. Even after Francis married again, the arrangement stood.

Thomas, Richard and Hugh formally signed over their claim to the administration of Henry's goods to Francis and as John had not been available added that,

*This wee no doubt not, but that our brother the Doctor in Oxford will be ready and willing to do.*

Poor Christopher also lost his wife, but this time as a result of being thrown from a horse. He never recovered from the shock and refused to marry again.

Thomas's son John could be secure in the knowledge that Stowford would belong to him on the death of his parents and the other children must either marry well or learn a trade in order to earn their living. Thomas and Blanche intended that their boys would also have a good property to live in and would not be allowing the extended family into any of the Stowford properties.

## 1639

The older generation remembered the style and majesty of Elizabeth's reign and so fell strongly behind the King. Others felt that taxation and law had become ridiculous and were for Parliament. Between 1629 and 1640 taxation levels were beyond a joke and despite the money raised, very little was being spent on the people of the land. In Devon and Cornwall the lack of investment in coastal defenses put the inhabitants under threat. Friends and neighbours were forced by their connection to government to collect default on taxes and confiscate their goods and livestock. These were then to be sold at auction, but no one would buy the goods in mutual allegiance and everything would be returned to their owners.

During this year, two siblings of Thomas Senior died. Aunt Agnes and Uncle Henry both died of a fever which ran through the community.

"What a ridiculous world we are living in," commented Thomas's eldest son John, now married and living at Bridgend with his wife Agnes. Hugh and Susan had married children of friends and lived locally. Thomas Junior was still living at home and becoming increasingly political in his beliefs. He had no intention of marrying, instead playing the field of willing local girls, who thought they might marry a Prideaux, should they manage to get 'caught.'

"Father is very upset that Professor John was not able to return from Oxford for their funerals. He is being kept under virtual house arrest and could not risk the journey," said Thomas.

"I think we should put up a plaque in the church in his honour and let the scoundrel Parliamentarians know whose side we are on. Then I am going to fight. Cousin

Arthur is raising a troop for the King and I am going to join it. What about you John?"

"I may, but someone has to stay here and make sure that the farm keeps running. Mother and Father are not as well as they were."

Thomas was unimpressed with this attitude and told him that the women could manage on their own. Any fighting would not last for long and could possibly be over by Christmas. They argued for a time as the two often did. But they agreed on a plaque and worded it carefully. The commission was given to their brother Hugh, to be completed without anyone else's knowledge. They knew that the Rector William Hart of Harford would not object to its being put up in the church, if for no other reason than the huge financial contributions the Prideaux family had made to its upkeep over the years.

When the finished article was hung in the main body of the church a month later, many came to look and admire. Thomas and Blanche were pleased although they told their boys that they should have been informed. Their neighbours thought that the Prideauxs were becoming more 'up' themselves by the day.

*Here rest the bodies of John Prideaux of Stoford and Agnes his only wife. The parents of [7] sonnes and [3] daughters.*

*To Whom*

*John Prideaux their 4<sup>th</sup> sonne Doctor of Divinity and their Kings Majesties Professour thereof in the University of Oxford Rector of Exceter Colledge and Chaplain to Prince Henry King James the first and King Charles the first*

*Hath left this filiall remembrance*

*July 20 1639*

**1640**

Thomas Prideaux Junior was becoming disillusioned with life 'at boring old Stowford' and informed his parents accordingly. He told his parents, Thomas and Blanche that he wanted to stay with his Uncle John and join him on his travels around Oxford and London.

"He has so much more fun than us down here. I mean, what was that with the witch trial? No one will tell me about it."

His mother changed the subject quickly. She accepted that for a man to be so high up in the Church as her brother in law was, he must deal with the dark side of life, the Devil included. But the rest of the family need not be involved. Everyone was well aware that Professor John had been chosen by King James to be chaplain and tutor to the heir apparent, Prince Henry and then Prince Charles. He had a wife and seven children and so many responsibilities and so much influence, that John Prideaux must be a safe advisor and companion for her precious son.

Blanche knew that she spoiled her petulant and argumentative son Thomas, but she thought she would lose him when he was born and felt responsible ever since. Her husband told her that she would 'turn him funny' the amount of time she spent with him and that she was the reason he still acted like a baby even though he was 31. Blanche ignored him, she had seen something in their son that reminded her of the ghostly old uncle who used to terrorise their home and worried that Thomas had somehow inherited his ghost. Naturally she told no one of this worry, for who would believe her?

Instead she kept a close eye on him ensuring that she could calm his more exuberant moods.

So Thomas had written to his Uncle John asking for permission to send young Thomas and received a positive response. There was a good deal of high spirits while plans were made and spare money collected and clothes cleaned and mended.

"When my brother John went to Oxford, he walked there in leather breeches and only food and a prayer book to sustain him on the road," Thomas informed his son.

"I've heard that story many times father and while I admire his tenacity, I shall not be walking to my Uncle's house. I shall be riding to Oxford." Thomas folded his arms across his chest in petulant defiance. Knowing looks passed between his father and mother.

However everything changed just before Thomas was about to leave, when a letter arrived at the house.

Thomas read it at the breakfast table.

"It seems that Uncle John has been accused of encouraging opposition in the University against the reforms of Archbishop Laud. His old pupil King Charles had to attend a hearing at Woodstock and apparently John has received a good telling off. The King though has said that John should not lose his place as he has been an honest servant to the Crown. Uncle John told the King that no man can be honest all the time. They laughed and apparently John was sent on his way. He says that although the King helped him out there and would ensure his safety, it is becoming increasingly apparent that there is trouble coming to this country and we must all be on our guard for spies. He thinks that there will come a time soon when brother shall be turned against brother."

"Well that all sounds very gloomy!" said Blanche, anxious to make light of the frightening letter.

"So, what about my trip to Oxford?" asked Thomas.

"My brother does not think that it will be safe for you just yet. He does not want to heighten the awareness of our family connections to Royalty. He says that soon allegiances will matter greatly. He said he will write only in an emergency as he cannot trust that his post is not being intercepted. He no longer tells people that he was born here, but in a different part of Devon altogether."

"Father, I am scared!" said Susan.

"Hush daughter, we shall be fine. We live too far from Parliament and the King. These politics shall not affect us, you'll see."

But Thomas was not nearly as sure as he sounded.

**1641**

Thomas Junior was conscious that his mother was becoming increasingly saddened and worried by the state of the county and the country as a whole. Arthur Prideaux at Ermington was raising a troop of horse for

King Charles and the Stowford Prideauxs agreed to help finance it in whatever way they could afford. Now that he was not allowed to go to Oxford, Thomas was adamant about joining the troop and fighting alongside three of his brothers. Thomas had still not married, considering this a ridiculous world in which to bring up children. His parents also knew that a marriage for Thomas Junior must necessarily mean that he must earn a living for a wife and family but currently he was too lazy and inconsistent to do that. Even so, neither Thomas nor Blanche wanted any of their sons to fight.

"Please don't let them go!" begged Blanche of her husband.

"The boys are grown men Blanche, they must make their own choices. Times are becoming too difficult and perhaps they will need to fight to save us all from ruin."

Thomas did not know how to answer his wife with any comforting words. He heard some terrible stories from his friends which he did not share with Blanche. He was keeping the stress of it all deep within him and had taken to walking and working away from the house as much as he could.

A few days later he met some strangers walking along the Highway. They were dressed in the easily recognisable garb of the Puritans. These people he knew would be travelling from Plymouth in the hope they could get some more ears to listen to their version of the Word of God. Thomas avoided them as a rule when similar people called at the house, instead sending a servant to force them on their way. These past years however, it was becoming increasingly obvious that these door knockers were in the game of obtaining information by gossip and observation to give to their associates if they felt that the Protestant scum were behaving against the Lord in any way.

That activity had been laughable and gossip worthy a few years ago, but lately there had been some repercussions. The words 'witch' and 'traitor' were being bandied about too often. Thomas knew from the experience of his brother John what that could mean. He had spoken to him about it on the Doctor's last trip home. John had told him to keep his head down and claim allegiance to no one.

"It's not a good world to be in at the moment, Thomas. There are strange energies and I believe there is a civil war coming. I know Cromwell and he actually believes his own publicity especially when it comes from the mouths of his agenda writing lackeys. He is a dangerous man who will kill people."

Thomas could not get the statement out of his head and he feared for his family and his land and his responsibilities.

"Are you a believer Sir?" asked one of the men.

Thomas stared at them and did not answer.

"Sir, we asked you a question. Are you a believer or a sinner?"

Thomas began to back up and called his dog to heel.

"There is evil standing with you Sir. What is your name? What is its name?"

A man in the group was pointing to the stone wall at the edge of the field and Thomas turned slowly around. He saw what he presumed the group saw, a hooded man waving a cane. This old man was making his way towards them in the jerkiest fashion, alternatively waving the cane in the air and falling to the ground. For someone who could only make such unusual movements he was making rapid progress towards them.

They froze as the thing came nearer to them, for as it was clearer to view, it was much more like a hooded demon with glowing eyes. Thomas half recognised it as the spirit he had seen in the library so long ago. But surely, this demon was more devil like, less human.

"It is the Devil!" shrieked one of the be-capped women as she staggered backwards.

The men rallied together in voice saying, "It is a familiar. This man is a witch. What is your name Sir? Are you from the Prideaux House?"

Thomas did not know whether he was more frightened of the cloaked scampering man or the group of Puritan snitches. Deciding that escape from this scenario was the best idea, Thomas began to run back to the house, wishing that there were not quite so many high stone walls around his fields. He pushed the scampering man out of his way as he heard from the group, "We shall inform our brothers and sisters of this. You will have to face trial and you will lose your home!"

Thomas felt as though he was running through treacle and he was fast losing his strength. He didn't feel out of breath nor did his legs feel weak. He was feeling lighter and lighter and – unusual. He felt as though his head was moving in front of his body and escaping it. It reminded him of swimming in deep water and he could sense the creature swimming towards him.

"Stop the world," someone shouted. "Thomas! Stop your world!"

His family found him dead in the Church Field when they went looking for him later that evening. He was alone and unmarked and there was a strange silver topped cane next to his body. Thomas's eyes and mouth were wide open, but there was no obvious cause of death.

## FOOTNOTES

The Prideaux Prayer;

**O God, That knowest us to bee set in the midst of so many and great dangers, that for Mans frailenesse we cannot always stand uprightly, guard to us the health of Body and Soul, that all those things which we suffer for sinne, by thy holy wee may well passé and overcome, through Jesus Christ our Lord.**

The Prayer has been handed down through the Prideaux family for centuries and was used almost as a spell in order to remove bad luck and serious illness. It was often used in times of plague. Bishop John Prideaux repeated it regularly and he had it recorded in many of his documents and published works. It features in **The Bishop and The Witch.** The prayer was used less as time went on and became forgotten and hidden away.

I found it.

I expect it still works.

The Will of Agnes Prideaux

The Will quoted and the codicil is the actual will of Agnes. I have copies of several Prideaux Family wills.

The Harford Church Memorial.

This Memorial to Bishop John Prideaux can be found in Harford Church. A local committee recently received funding which they used for the restoration of the plaque.

# THE ERMINGTON CURSE

## Featuring Thomas and Joane Prideaux of Stowford and Ermington

One day during May 1641, when his brothers were making preparations to join Arthur Prideaux over at Ermington for a meeting, Thomas Junior burst in to the kitchen at Prideaux House and announced,

"There is a document we must all sign or be seen to sign and God knows what that means!"

"Thomas! Do not take the Lord's name in vain!" said his mother in a shocked voice. Since her husband's death, Blanche had had a visit from Puritan elders informing her that they believed her husband to be a Devil worshipper and that the Prideaux family must change their ways. Now it was certain that the family was being watched and their actions recorded.

"I apologise mother, but this is serious." Thomas threw one of the chairs across the kitchen in a flash of temper – he had been doing that a lot lately.

It seemed that they were all to sign a document which stated that they would be loyal to the King and the rights and privileges of Parliament and to uphold the true Protestant religion. Thomas was finding it difficult to take this constant pressure and worry and was recently veering from serious anger issues to total collapse.

Fearful that signing the documents would make them eligible for something for which   they did not wish to be eligible and failing to sign and being branded a Catholic and losing their lands, made for tense times. The neighbourhood was forced to travel directly to Ivybridge on a summoned day in May and sign the Returns. The Prideaux men, Francis, Henry, Hugh, James, John, Richard, Simon and Thomas all signed along with their neighbours.

This done, there was a heightened sense of persecution. Thomas particularly became edgy and his already short temper became nastier. He was obsessing about his Uncle John and the news that his sons were fighting for the King. Thomas became enraged yet again and began smashing a shovel around the courtyard. His brother John had taken over the house since his father's death and was constantly encouraging Thomas to get married, get a job, do anything – just leave.

Thomas ignored him.

When a parliamentary rebellion began in South Devon, Hopton arrived to help crush it, much to the excitement of the Prideaux men and their cousins. This news inspired them to travel to Modbury with Arthur

Prideaux to join the posse. The crowd excitement as they waited for the great Sir Ralph Hopton made the whole day seem more like a village fair than a posse. Friends joshed each other and pushed each other around and compared pikes and staffs.

The Prideaux men owned guns and were part of only twenty men so armed. They also owned riding horses and were able to ride to Modbury. Although they were equally excited by the general air of joviality, they were dismayed to see that there was no discipline amongst the men at all. The rabble drank and argued and would listen to nothing they were told in respect of planning for battle. They were keen on the idea of fighting and defending their neighbourhood, but once together in a group they only wanted to party.

Before the motley group was ready, an army of Parliament men quietly moved on the town of Modbury and the unarmed rustics fled for their lives. The Fortescues and Henry Champernowne were captured while all the Prideauxs managed to escape.

"This is dangerous," they said to each other as they galloped back to Stowford vowing not to tell the women just how bad things were becoming.

They kept their heads down for many months, working on the farm and engaging with only a few trusted souls. It was almost impossible to tell who was for the King and who for Cromwell. And it was too dangerous not to know.

Most of the Prideaux family was coping with this way of living, but Thomas found it stressful and difficult and was suffering from tense, angry outbursts interspersed with panic attacks. He was also suffering from bad dreams and hallucinations. Blanche was worried about her son, but then she always had been. Now he was telling her that he could see his father and his grandfather walking around the farm and that he had seen a tall hooded man beckoning to him with a cane. She told him to keep it to himself.

In spite of civil war breaking out all across the country, the men of the south west only came out to fight again in 1643, when there was another attack on the neighbourhood. This time there was hand to hand fighting in the streets of Modbury for many days and there were too many deaths on both sides. The Royalists eventually had to retreat under attack at all boundaries of the town by the Roundheads.

Thomas Prideaux was amongst the soldiers for the Royalist cause and one day he took a rest from the fighting by sitting on an oak bench hidden by shrubbery in the garden of a house just off the main street. Although most of the townspeople had fled, some were still hiding in their houses. As Thomas leant against the side of the house, he heard a voice from the window above him.

"Are you alright?"

Thomas looked up and saw the most beautiful girl he had ever seen, looking out of the window. He felt slightly foolish now that he was cowering behind a bush trying to drink some home whisky from a flask he held in his hand.

"Not really. I have just killed two men I know."

"Oh! What happened?"

"They killed my horse!"

"Well they deserved it," said the girl. "Had you had the horse long?"

"I reared him from a foal and I bred his mother and father and they just killed him and it took ages for him to die. I almost can't bear it." Thomas suddenly felt ashamed for declaring this weakness to a complete stranger. He got up quickly and made to leave.

"Please don't go just yet," she said. "Stay a moment and get your wits back. Would you like to come in and rest?" she added.

"No!" he answered horrified. To go inside a house and rest would be seen as cowardly. But his second thought was the acknowledgement that leaving the fight was exactly what he wanted to do and so he went into her cottage. Thomas was glad to sit down again.

"What is your name?" he asked.

"I am Joane Fox."

"Pleased to meet you Joane Fox, I am Thomas Prideaux of Stowford."

"I know of your family. I am pleased to meet you Thomas Prideaux."

Thomas stood up again and smiled at his new friend. He said with renewed confidence,

"I shall not forget your kindness to me Joane. I shall come back and find you when this fighting is over. Now go and make sure you keep yourself safe."

She rewarded him with a beautiful smile.

"Are you alone in the house?"

"My father is out fighting in the town somewhere. My mother and I are keeping everything safe here."

"Do you have brothers and sisters?"

"No, just father, mother and me."

Thomas was surprised to realise that although he was living amongst death and destruction, he was still pleased to hear that the owner of this lovely face was not married. Better than that, it appeared this lovely face, although a little manly but he liked manly, was sole heir to this house and land. She would do.

The war continued for too many more years and meant a great loss of fortune for the Stowford Prideauxs. Occupation of this area changed hands several times and in some cases people changed their names in order to stay safe. Neighbours were informing on their neighbours and everyone became very different people. Almost no conversations of substance took place and old arguments were surfacing and terrible revenges were being exacted.

It was almost impossible to make money when the men could not tend the stock and fields, leaving this work to the ever capable womenfolk. The markets were often closed and food and animals were demanded by the armies, whichever army was occupying the farmland at the time. Blanche heard on more than one occasion,

"Mistress Prideaux. Who is the tall hooded man I have seen running through the woods? I fear he would attack me until I fired a shot in his direction."

"I know not Sir," she would answer. "He is not known to us."

Thomas no longer was ridiculed for his ghostly hallucinations as many were seeing spirits of the dead from both sides. It seemed that many recently killed sons and fathers were appearing back at their nearby homes informing their families that they were home for good, only for the same families to learn that at that exact moment he had taken a fatal blow of some sort and the family must go and fetch the body from a collection point in Modbury.

Thomas himself had seen the ghosts of the only two men he had killed. He was at root a coward, but he did love his horses. The ghosts he constantly saw, so recently and so long dead, were not helping his nerves and his excursions between temper and nerves were regular.

One morning he called round to see his brother John at Stowford.

The King had been executed and Thomas now had Woodlands Farm, due to some of the confiscations. He had acquired it from a Prideaux cousin whose branch of the family had occupied the property for three hundred years. Woodlands was situated on land to the south of the Highway and south west of the Ivy Bridge. As with the Stowford Manor and Prideaux land, the Ivy Bridge had a corner on all of their properties. The fourth corner was on land known as Pitt. If the Williams family and the two Prideauxs all stood in the corner of their lands, they could all touch the bridge. These landowners were under obligation to grind their corn at the mills owned by the Williams family which were situated on the Stowford bank.

"John," Thomas said as he entered the familiar kitchen. Although all the children had married and left home, they still treated Stowford as their own home and their brother John and his wife Agnes always made them welcome.

"Hello Thomas, come and sit down. Agnes, make Thomas some food and drink."

Agnes put down her baby and went over to the stove.

"How are Joane and little James?" she asked.

"Fine Agnes, fine. James is turning out to be a fat little baby and Joane spends all her time with him."

"So she should. After losing her mother and father in the fighting, she will want to keep hanging on to the baby."

"I know, that is why she wanted to call him James after her father. We will call the next one Thomas."

"But the property is coming to you though? To her?" John turned to glare at Agnes, the private conversations they had between them about Thomas marrying Joane for her money he did not want voicing outwardly.

Thomas looked at her and answered, "Of course the property and estate is mine. It is my right."

"It is hard to believe how many family and friends have died during the last few years," said Agnes, hoping to change the subject.

"Some from fighting and some from being worn out with worry," reminisced Thomas.

"Bishop John has fared the worst, losing all his five sons and his bishopric. They still consult him apparently, but he now has little fortune and lives with one of his daughters in a small parsonage in Bredon, I think."

"He wrote and said that he is trying to write down everything he has experienced in his life – it should be quite a tale. He is fading fast, what a way to end an important life."

"Leading that life put him in the firing line and perhaps us too, Thomas."

"What do you mean John?"

"You are to lose Woodland Farm, Thomas. The place has been confiscated again and sold and the new man is a Cromwell man who does not approve of us. Too many Royal connections he said."

"What about Joane's properties?"

"Those are currently safe and we must allow the lawyers to do their work."

"When did you find this out, brother of mine?" Thomas was standing now and menacing John with his fist.

John patted the air with his hands, trying to calm his volatile brother.

"I have spoken to Cousin Thomas at Ermington and he has found you a cottage there."

"But we have another baby on the way, Joane will be devastated!"

"There is nothing to be done, believe me I have tried very hard."

He watched Thomas shake and spill his drink. Ever since the fighting, Thomas had become harder to deal with. Seeing all the death and living under stress for so long had affected him badly. His temper was becoming worse and his family would tread carefully around him when he was particularly tense.

Thomas could not make decisions easily and John had kept the news of the loss from him until something had been sorted out, unacceptable as it might have been, at least it was something. It had been left to John to sort out most of the family's problems as heir and Thomas was not good at sorting out his own issues.

"I am sorry Thomas, I have done the best I can for your family. We are sorry that you are to lose your family home and it is heartbreaking. I am however trying to keep Prideaux family money and belongings together and I have a few schemes up my sleeve for that."

"But you are allowing them to take our home?"

"I am doing the best I can. Please don't criticise me."

Times were so difficult. When their Uncle Richard had died in 1645 and his wife Elizabeth a year later, the bulk of their property was left to Thomas Williams at Stowford in order to safeguard it from the government. So many neighbours helped each other out in order to protect lives and property. Sometimes John felt as though his head would explode while Thomas just seemed to ignore everything that was happening.

Agnes stood and watched the brothers carefully. She knew that Thomas may erupt explosively but she loved him as a brother who had experienced much and she considered his wife Joane a sister. She also knew that the Williams family appeared to be ignoring the safeguarding aspect of the Prideaux legacy and were refusing to return it to the family. This meant that the Williams now owned the land across the road and to the north west of their farm. The gardens had been landscaped in Elizabeth's time in her honour and were visited and enjoyed by local and visiting dignitaries alike. If Thomas learnt of that too, he would probably go to them and do something which would require a hanging.

John Prideaux must keep calm.

"You have to leave Thomas, for your family's safety."

Thomas dropped his fist and became almost rigid. John escorted him back to his horse which was tethered in the courtyard and patted his shoulders.

"It will work out fine Thomas, you see."

Thomas turned to him and said, "I shall never forgive you John, for this. Our ancestors will curse you and this property and haunt you to your death."

"Don't be silly Thomas," said Agnes.

As Thomas rode away towards Ivybridge John turned to his wife, "Better get the Rector Hart in to bless the place. Just in case."

Agnes nodded and walked back inside.

On a misty morning in May 1649, Thomas and Joane left Woodland for Ermington with baby James. Their cousin Thomas Prideaux from Ermington had found them a decent property which sat opposite the church and the rent from which would have to be paid to the church.

James had been christened there rather than Modbury or Harford in order to confuse gossips.

Thomas slammed down his bag and walking stick in the new hallway and turned to his wife and said,

"I am ashamed to bring you to this place Joane. I never thought it would come to this."

"Not to worry Thomas, let's make the best of it, we shall be on our feet in no time, you see."

"I think I shall rest upstairs as soon as the bed has been laid out, you carry on organising the house my dear. I am feeling very shaky and tired."

Joane sighed. Really her husband was becoming most tiresome of late. Always nervy and cross and then tired and depressed. Why am I supposed to have more energy than him? He is only 39 and I have been through a lot too.

The walking stick was a new addition. Thomas said it made him feel secure as recently his legs were prone to giving way.

She shouted James into the kitchen and met the maids and set them about their work. As soon as the inheritance from her family property came through, she intended to invest in other property and secure a rental income from that. In the meantime she would use the meagre savings she had kept from her lazy husband and keep the family safe.

But two years passed all too quickly, their second son Andrew had been born and another child on the way. Bishop John was dead and Cromwell was still in charge of the country.

"Any news about the money yet my dear?" she asked her husband at breakfast one morning. The lawyers were dealing with Thomas and not her, even though the inheritance was coming from her side of the family. He told her that the Parliamentarians were being shady and not allowing the money to change hands. This was not true and Thomas already had the quite substantial inheritance sitting in his own bank.

"Don't worry me about such things Joane. Get on with your responsibilities and leave me to mine. I have several plans in motion already. You are only a woman, you would not understand."

Joane said nothing, feeling the familiar heaviness of depression. This pregnancy was getting her down more than the other two and she vowed that this would be the last child she would produce for this family. She would make sure that she would keep her cool until the money came and then things would change. She was trying desperately not to hate the life growing inside her and holding her back from freedom.

Thomas felt a little giddy again.

*I would have told her that the money had come through, he said to himself, but honestly I do not have the strength to discuss it at the moment. I shall keep it in the bank and think about it later.*

He got up from the breakfast table, taking up the cane he had rescued from beside the body of his father and went to the front door in order to go out for a walk.

He opened the door and the blast of cold air made him feel very jumpy.

*I am still weak, he thought. I shall go back to bed* and he turned and made his way upstairs.

*Someone else will sort things out.*

\*

*If I was actually going mad, would I know that I was? I don't really know what the rules are about that. I can't ask anyone about it because I could be locked up. Staring out of the window in my cottage in Ermington, I can see my boys running up the bank towards the church. They are laughing and joking and pushing each other over into the grass. Peter, the youngest boy looks as though he will cry sometimes but when Andrew and James pull him up and chase him again, he seems to forget about crying. I wish I could forget about crying. I feel so tired and ill. My legs are like lead weights and sometimes it is all I can do to walk across the room, let alone go out and work. But just lately things seem to have been getting worse.*

"Mr. Prideaux," Ellen, the servant girl said as she entered the room. "What am I supposed to be making for supper?"

"Can't you sort that out yourself? I have enough on my mind."

"Well alright, but I just was wondering if you had any special thing you wanted. Not that there is much to choose from. I mean I am a good cook, but I think it would help if you gave me a bit more money so that I could buy more things from Mrs. Lane."

*Does the woman not know how much I do not care about that? I am here with my mind going away from me, voices screaming, screaming, screaming and the stupid servant thinks that what she says is important.*

"Make whatever the boys like best. I am not interested in eating today,"

Ellen screwed up her face, turned on her heel and stalked out of the room.

*I return to my task of looking out of the window. I can only see two boys now and they are standing by the well next to the church. Annie Applecart is standing by them talking away. I don't think that is really her name, but that is what I shall call her.*

Ellen stormed into the room again, causing the door to swing violently on its hinges.

"That witch is with the boys Mr. Prideaux. Shall I fetch them back?"

"You shouldn't call her a witch because that kind of talk gets innocent people into trouble."

"She is a witch, everyone knows that. I am not frightened to tell the truth! Anyway, am I to fetch the boys back or not?"

*She had her hands on her hips and as I look at her I feel dizzy and peculiar. What on earth is the matter with me?*

"The boys are fine. The truth is that I don't want the boys hanging around the house screaming and shouting. Their voices go through my brain, cutting it to shreds."

*Now I think I shall put my papers in order again. I did it yesterday but I am not sure whether Ellen upset the order when she cleaned this morning. Although she calls it cleaning, I would not. I notice that there are cobwebs hanging from the beams.*

"If we have spiders, we won't have flies," she told me.

*I don't want either flies or spiders. Mice or rats for that matter will not be welcome as far as I am concerned. The crashing noise Ellen is making in the kitchen is driving me crackers. No not crackers, it is making me angry. Crash, bash and smash. Thank you for that. Oh not this, why should this be the letter which comes first in the pile? Now I will have to read it again three times and take away its power.*

**My dear new baby,**

**I am concerned that I may not be with you travelling the path of life. God has told me that I am needed with him earlier than I ever planned. I have reconciled myself to this, but am determined that I shall bring you into the world and allow you the chance to experience everything that this wonderful life has to offer. I have already grown to love you and never want you to feel that you will have missed out on knowing me. I shall ask Jesus to let me watch over you and help you on your way. I will watch over my Andrew and James too. Your father is a good man and will make sure that you will have all the love and support that you require. Your path in life can be short or long, good or bad but it is up to you to ensure that you are kind and loving whenever you can be.**

**Joane your loving Mother.**

*Yes, well done Joane, you got to go and live with Jesus and left me with the looking after them all. I think that was a very selfish thing for you to have done.*

*"Give this letter to the new baby," I remember you said. Well what good will that do? He can't read yet!*

"Mr. Prideaux, I think we should get those boys back in here now. It is nearly suppertime and I don't like them being near that woman."

*I go to the window again and can still see the two eldest boys playing by the well. Annie is sitting on the grass talking to them. Who is that standing behind her? A man dressed in a long black coat and wearing a tall black hat. I never saw anyone dressed like that in my life. It is very odd.*

"I would be more worried about the man standing with them," I answered. "I have never seen him before."

"I don't know anything about a man. I didn't see a man standing anywhere near them." Ellen was used to her master's funny ways. "So am I fetching the boys back in?"

*I don't know why everything has to be so complicated.*

"Yes go and fetch them in." I instructed.

*I go back to the window and watch Ellen leave by the gate and march over the lane and up the bank towards the field. She seems undecided about whether or not to walk up the church track or go through the gate. Decision made, she tries the field gate and finding it immovable, lifts up her skirts and climbs over the wooden structure.*

*The two boys look up as Ellen strode up the field and Annie stood up. Neither little Peter nor the odd looking man are anywhere to be seen. As Ellen reaches the gathering she walks straight over to Annie and appears to punch her in the face. Annie fell to the ground whatever had happened. The boys run over to Annie to help but then stop and follow Ellen. She must have told them to leave the girl alone. I still can't see where Peter is. Now Ellen has her hands on her hips and is turning and shouting. After a while she moves over to the well, looks over the edge and then screams at the boys, who both now are running down the hill towards the cottage.*

*Transfixed, I watch them clamber over the gate and cross the road without looking. A man driving a pony and cart shouted at them to get out of his way. Ellen will not be pleased about that. Suddenly they are at my window jumping up and down and shouting.*

"Father, Father! You must come quickly. Peter has fallen down the well!"

*Really this is too much. What am I supposed to do about it? I can't climb down a well, or back up one for that matter. The boys have given up banging on the window and have come running into the house and up to my room.*

"Father, did you not hear us? Peter has fallen down the well and Ellen says that you must come straight away!"

"Don't bother me now boys, I have such a headache. I am very tired and am sure that I could not make it up to the top of the hill. You must sort out your own problems."

"But father, he might die!" shouted James. At almost fifteen years old, James was grown up and he certainly was not shy about shouting at his father.

"Don't be so dramatic boy. I have to consider my health, your shouting has upset me you bad boy, I must go and lie down."

*I only just made it to the chair by the fire. I don't know why they are still in the room. James and Andrew soon give up annoying me and leave. I feel so dizzy and my heart is racing. I can feel it banging against my chest. I can't decide whether or not I have a brain growth or am about to have a heart attack. I just know I can hardly lift my arms and have dark spots in front of my eyes. I must rest them now.*

"Mr. Prideaux, wake up. Come on, wake up."

*I open my eyes and see the doctor looking at me. He seems angry, not worried. Stupid man.*

"So glad that you came to see me George. I have been feeling very poorly today."

"I am not interested in how you are feeling. We have put your son into his bed. He has a broken leg. I have set it as well as I can and we must watch him carefully over the next few weeks. He is lucky to be alive."

"Who has a broken leg?"

"Young Peter."

"How has that happened?"

*I don't understand these people. Can't they see that I am the one who is ill?*

"He fell down the well. Can you not remember?"

"I am tired. I need to sleep," I answer.

"You need to take hold of your responsibilities and look after your family properly," shouted the Doctor. "We are all well aware of the troubles you have had in your life, but now you must move on. Your family needs you."

*I close my eyes. I can still hear, but now the group in the room seems to be leaving me alone. This dark swirling which happens when I close my eyes is very unnerving. I lose my grip on the reality in which everyone else lives and feel as though I am falling down a deep dark hole, but spinning the entire time. It is so sickly and frightening. Joane my beautiful dead wife, I miss you so much. Perhaps if I reach out my hand I can touch you my darling. So nice of you to visit every time I have one of these spells. Does that mean I am dead too when this happens? Who knows? Who cares? When I see you, I remember how I got into this state. Shall I think about it again my love? Perhaps I shall improve when I do.*

*I feel as though I cannot take any more. When we arrived at this house, I was appalled. We now had a small front garden and two servants. There are only four rooms downstairs and four up. There is some land and buildings out the back, but really it is a disgrace.*

*Joane, you said that we must make the best of it and I really tried to settle in with the few possessions we had been allowed to take.*

*For a Prideaux to be in this position is wrong. My brothers have fared little better and it seems now that it will be down to our cousins to carry on the fame and fortune of our family name. It would not surprise me if they had not made advancement from the situation we find ourselves in.*

*We were only here for two weeks when Joane started with the baby. We had endured looks and comments from the new neighbors, who appeared to find it amusing that we were in this position. Joane took it all very well even though I wanted to cause some trouble.*

*I started to feel ill about this time. My heart raced and I felt peculiar when walking along the street. Nerves said my wife. I told her that was ridiculous. Nerves are a female trouble; it must be something more serious.*

*Her labour lasted for two days and Joane was in great distress. She was attended by Ellen and a woman from the village. Our own doctor could not of course come and see her and there was no doctor in the village at that time.*

*My lovely wife died and the boy survived. I know it was not Peter that killed her, but she died because of him all the same.*

*Ellen found a wet nurse for the boy and I buried my wife in the churchyard at Ermington. She should have been buried at Harford, along with my own parents and family, or at Modbury with her parents, but at least I can see her every time I look out of my windows at the front of the house.*

*From that point on, I often felt as though I could no longer cope. I knew that all the people in the village would look at me. Ellen said it was in sympathy, but I knew the truth. They thought that I had some hand in the death of my wife!*

*Peter, I have never felt close to. Andrew and James are not so bad, but Peter wants to annoy me at every opportunity. When the other boys were babies, they were well out of sight with their maids while we carried on with our lives. In fact I suppose I hardly ever saw them except for bedtimes and playing in the garden. Now all the children are within my eyesight and earshot every moment of the day. I had not really been aware of the noise and smell involved with a new baby. I even caught the wet nurse feeding the boy on several occasions. Disgusting. When I was a child, all of this was carried on in the babies' nursery away from us all.*

"Mr. Prideaux, Mr. Prideaux!"

*I am being shaken about by Ellen.*

"What on earth is the matter with you girl?"

*I open my eyes and see that I am still lying on the sofa in the sitting room. It is daylight. I must have slept through the night.*

"I thought you were dead Mr. Prideaux. You've slept all yesterday and today!" Ellen could not believe that anyone would sleep that long.

"I am ill, I keep telling you. Now go and get me some wine."

"Wine! We don't have wine. You are not in your big house now."

"Don't be so rude you dreadful girl, or I shall dismiss you!"

"You know you won't do any such thing. There is no one else that will put up with you. Anyway I am not leaving those boys. You aren't fit to look after them." Ellen was nothing if not confident.

*I lay back on my couch and then realise that I must visit the outside privy immediately. Oh how the room spins and turns. The floor is moving and I am sure that I shall die.*

"Ellen, Ellen! Come quickly and bring my po!"

"Mr. Prideaux, you are a disgrace. There is nothing wrong with you. The po is under the couch same as before. Now when you have done that, clean yourself up and go and visit your poor boy." She bustled back into the kitchen.

*I did as I was told and was soon standing in the hallway looking up the stairs wondering if I could make it. It takes me such a long time, but on seeing my boy, I almost feel sorry for him.*

"Hello Father," he said.

"Hello Peter. What happened to you?"

"I fell down the well. I don't know how Sir, I was talking to that man and next thing I knew I was down the well."

"You saw the man too? No one else seems to have done."

"I know, Andrew and James said they didn't see him either. He said he knew our family. But it was very odd because he would not say who he was."

*I look down at my eleven year old son. He seems so much younger than his thirteen and fifteen year old brothers, more like a baby. I suppose that is because he is sick.*

"I am sick too," I said out loud.

"Oh," answered Peter.

*I know he finds me strange, we have never been close.*

"So tell me about this man," I asked.

"Better tell your father about that witch woman." Ellen had come into the room behind us.

"She's not really a witch Ellen. She's nice to me. She teaches me things," said Peter.

"What sort of things, may I ask? I can't see that she could teach you anything that will be any good to you in the long run. Pity you didn't pay as much attention to your tutor," answered Ellen curtly.

*I know full well that Ellen has a crush on Mr. Grayling who comes to the house every day to teach the boys.*

"She teaches me about plants and animals. You know, about herbs and things which can make people better," said Peter.

*That was surprising as I had not been aware that Peter was learning anything from anyone. Certainly Mr. Grayling was not that pleased with the boy's progress.*

"I don't know what use that could possibly be," I said.

Peter could be cheeky when he found his confidence.

"For example, Annie showed me a way we could help you with your nerves."

*I gave Peter no chance to elaborate.*

"You have been discussing my health with that witch! My illness is far too complicated for a pair of idiots such as you two to cure. Why, I have baffled greater brains than yours!"

*As I leave the room, I notice Ellen standing in the hallway still. Peter has a crestfallen face and it serves him right. I gave him, a parting shot.*

"Pity she didn't know a way to save your mother before you killed her!"

*His face shows that this has hit home. He won't be giving me any of his ridiculous advice from now on.*

"Mr. Prideaux! There was no call for that!" said Ellen.

*I feel ill again. My legs are wobbling and the whole situation is too much for me. I shall retire to my bed.*

*

*I don't know why I have just been thinking about Peter and his broken leg. It must be 29 years since that happened.*

"Now Mr. Prideaux, we need to get you washed and changed before your lawyer gets here."

*Ellen left us years ago. She was followed by a long succession of housekeepers and maids and now I have this dragon of a woman to look after me. She does seem to understand how ill I am though, which is something. I don't know what the Lord is playing at, leaving me so poorly for so long. At one time I could not travel far from the house and now I am unable to leave my bed. The best doctors are baffled and one gentleman wanted to study me saying that it would be a revelation to discover how a man who showed no outward or inward signs of illness could be so sick! I said to him, it is for you to discover that. I am too busy trying to keep my life together when so many things have been against me.*

"That's right, move over so we can wash your face and trim your whiskers. Really you are so lucky to keep such a fine head of hair, when most men of your age have lost theirs!"

"Where are my children, Miss Traeth?"

"Well James is at his home, I should imagine. Remember he has married that nice Sarah Cope and they have the two babies, Sarah and Agnes?"

"Oh yes. It had slipped my mind just for the moment."

*It is true to say that many things are easily forgotten by my poorly mind.*

"Andrew is courting Joan Wake, but she will have a job getting him to the altar and Peter! Well I will be surprised if he ever marries! Too fond of himself that one."

"Peter has been trouble since the day he came into the world. He killed my beautiful Joane, just when I needed her to look after me. It really is too much."

"No need to talk about your flesh and blood like that, Mr. Prideaux. You are lucky to have such good healthy sons and grandchildren. I wish I had."

*She busies herself nursing me and sorting out the bed and the room. I can hear some commotion downstairs and soon my lawyer, Mr. Kidling arrives.*

"You are looking very well Thomas! You should be up and about today, the sun is glorious."

"No need for enforced joviality George. Have you prepared the documents?"

"Yes I have and just as you asked. The boys will be very pleased with the amount of money and property you are leaving in your estate."

"I have never thought about spending much money, it was not necessary. I managed to come out of the disaster of Cromwell with more than anyone expected and have kept it invested since then."

"Indeed you have. The will splits the money equally between the boys and if any die before you, then the balance shall be divided between the surviving sons."

"Exactly right."

"Now my clerk and Miss Traeth can witness your signature. There and there and there. I shall take this back to my office and keep it safe. Good day to you Thomas."

"Good day to you George."

"Hello Peter, I did not realize you were on the landing." The lawyer shook his hand.

"Neither did I Peter. What are you doing there? Trying to discover something which is of no concern of yours?"

"No indeed Father. I came to see if you wanted anything from Modbury. I am travelling there today."

"To see your gambling friends I have no doubt. I am dismayed by the amount of money you waste in that game."

"I know I have been a constant disappointment to you Sir. I am sorry for that. Do you want anything then?"

"No I don't. I need to rest now."

*

"It's terrible sad about losing your brother and father within the same month, Peter."

"Yes it is Miss Traeth."

"Just before Christmas too. I mean poor James dying of food poisoning and the same with your father."

"I don't think Father died of food poisoning. He has been ill for so long, it should be no surprise that he passed soon after James. He was his favorite son after all. The final shock I suppose."

Andrew came over to join them and Miss Traeth left to see to the other guests.

"It is rather odd though Peter. I have been used to father being ill all our life, I can't believe he is really dead."

"I know Andrew, but I am more amazed by James dying, than father. I worry for his poor wife and children. I hope that they will cope."

"We shall have to share some of our inheritance with them, so that they will be able to manage."

"You can if you like Andrew. Father insisted that the money was shared between his remaining sons. He never mentioned anything about providing for James's wife and children. It is father who is to blame for that little oversight."

"Peter you can't possibly mean that! James would have looked after any family of ours."

"We don't have any family, that's the point."

"If you won't share yours, then I shall share mine with them!"

"That is up to you. My father has hated me since the day I was born and he let me know it almost every day. He hid his money from us all and let us live like paupers. With our background and history, that was awful. We could have lived well ever since Mother's old place had to be given up. I was very angry as soon as I heard about the money. Perhaps mother would even have lived if she had been attended by a proper doctor."

"You only heard about it the same time as me though, didn't you? At the reading of the will?"

"Oh yes that's right, at the reading of the will. Anyway, I am going to finally enjoy my life and marry a rich woman and have sons. I will start another Prideaux dynasty and climb my way back up the ladder. We shall have our position back Andrew and that is not going to happen by giving our money away. After all, Sarah is only the daughter of a parson!"

"You didn't mind seeing the daughter of a stonemason last week. What happened to her?"

"That was just something to pass the time. I am aiming for bigger fish now."

"I am ashamed of you Peter."

"Do I look as though I care Andrew? We shall keep this house for you and I shall buy that new house at the end of the village and buy new clothes and horses. You can buy me out, I won't be coming back here. Soon I shall take my rightful place. You watch, Andrew, You watch!"

"Mother would be ashamed of you too!"

"Leave me now, I have to visit old Annie and give her a Christmas present. She has always been good to me."

*

"Oh how pleased I am to see you Peter! Come on in."

"Thanks Annie." He sat by the fire and took the drink which Annie handed to him.

"Now do you want something to eat?"

"No thanks. I am content to sit here."

Annie sat opposite him and played with her cup, obviously wondering whether or not to say something to him. She decided to.

"I was worried you would not visit after the death of your father."

"Why would you think that?"

"Because of how he died."

Peter looked at her sharply.

"What do you mean by that?"

"It seems a mighty coincidence that your brother and father both died within a month of your learning about your father's will. They both died by poisoning too."

"James died from poisoning and Father died of shock."

"Stick to that story, it doesn't matter to me. It will never come from my lips that you know as much as me when it comes to herbs and plants and the effects they have on people."

Peter grabbed her by the arm,

"Don't ever let me hear you saying anything like that to anyone else."

Annie looked him in the eyes and smiled.

"Oh Peter, we have meant a lot to each other over the years, you know I never want you to be in trouble."

"I won't be in trouble, but you might if you don't leave me alone. Witches are still burnt you know. It would not take much for the village to be fired up, especially if I let them know about your spells and curses."

"Peter! Why would you do that?"

"Because you are a witch! And you are accusing me of harming my family. We still have a witch bottle in our fireplace. Ellen put it there years ago and I know quite a few others have them too. They believe your mother was a witch and that you are too."

"I can't believe you are saying this to me after all we have meant to each other."

Peter stood up and slapped the woman hard across the face.

"We are nothing to each other. I have money now and am going to make something of my life. You can't hurt me, our family has been too powerful for anything you say or do to affect us. A curse wouldn't even work on me."

Annie was slumped on the floor and crying.

"Don't bother me again. Don't come near me or I shall have you flogged and burned as a witch!"

Peter stared at her with his black eyes and then abruptly left her cottage.

"I know you were affected by your father's coldness, but you had every chance to remain good and not turn evil."

She turned over the little doll in her hand. She had made it years ago when Peter first kissed her because she knew this day would come.

"You will never have luck with money or love Peter Prideaux and your children and your children's' children will suffer the same unless the curse is broken. Not so clever are you?"

She threw the doll on the fire and laughed.

"So there you are fire, hold the secret."

Annie looked out of the doorway at the retreating Peter Prideaux.

"Bastard," she said.

If you want to follow the adventures of Peter and his descendants, then look out for the next books of Prideaux Ghost Stories which will be published over the coming months.

www.ingramcontent.com/pod-product-compliance
Lightning Source LLC
Chambersburg PA
CBHW051946170626
46808CB00007B/2508